s

BURNING
BRIGHT

HARD TIMES

Jacob stood in the barn mouth and watched Edna leave the henhouse. Her lips were pressed tight, which meant more eggs had been taken. He looked up at the ridgetop and guessed eight o'clock. In Boone it'd be full morning now, but here light was still splotchy and dew damped his brogans. This cove's so damn dark a man about has to break light with a crowbar, his daddy used to say.

Edna nodded at the egg pail in her hand.

"Nothing under the bantam," Edna said. "That's four days in a row."

"Maybe that old rooster ain't sweet on her no

more," Jacob said. He waited for her to smile. When they'd first started sparking years ago, Edna's smile had been what most entranced him. Her whole face would glow, as if the upward turn of her lips spread a wave of light from mouth to forehead.

"Go ahead and make a joke," she said, "but little cash money as we got it makes a difference. Maybe the difference of whether you have a nickel to waste on a newspaper."

"There's many folks worse off," Jacob said. "Just look up the cove and you'll see the truth of that."

"We can end up like Hartley yet," Edna replied. She looked past Jacob to where the road ended and the skid trail left by the logging company began. "It's probably his mangy hound that's stealing our eggs. That dog's got the look of a egg-sucker. It's always skulking around here."

"You don't know that. I still think a dog would leave some egg on the straw. I've never seen one that didn't."

"What else would take just a few eggs at a time? You said your ownself a fox or weasel would have killed the chickens."

"I'll go look," Jacob said, knowing Edna would fret over the lost eggs all day. He knew if every hen laid three eggs a night for the next month, it wouldn't matter. She'd still perceive a debit that would never be made up. Jacob tried to be generous, remembered that Edna hadn't always been this way. Not until the bank had taken the truck and most of the livestock. They hadn't lost everything the way others had, but they'd lost enough. Edna always seemed fearful when she heard a vehicle coming up the dirt road, as if the banker and sheriff were coming to take the rest.

Edna carried the eggs to the springhouse as Jacob crossed the yard and entered the concrete henhouse. The smell of manure thickened the air. Though the rooster was already outside, the hens clucked dimly in their nesting boxes. Jacob lifted the bantam and set it on the floor. The nesting box's straw had no shell crumbs, no albumen or yellow yolk slobber.

He knew it could be a two-legged varmint, but hard as times were Jacob had never known anyone in Goshen Cove to steal, especially Hartley, the poorest of them all. Besides, who would take only two or three eggs when there were two dozen more to be had. The bantam's eggs at that, which were smaller than the ones under the Rhode Island Reds and leghorns. From the barn, Jacob heard the Guernsey lowing insistently. He knew she already waited beside the milk stool.

As Jacob came out of the henhouse he saw the Hartleys coming down the skid trail. They made the two-mile trek to Boone twice a week, each, even the child, burdened down with galax leaves. Jacob watched as they stepped onto the road, puffs of gray dust rising around their bare feet. Hartley carried four burlap pokes stuffed with galax. His wife carried two and the child one. With their ragged clothes hanging loose on bony frames, they looked like scarecrows en route to another cornfield, their possessions in tow. The hound trailed them, gaunt as the people it followed. The galax leaves were the closest thing to a crop Hartley could muster, for his land was all rock and slant. You couldn't grow a toenail on Hartley's land, Bascombe Lindsey had once said. That hadn't been a problem as long as the sawmill was running, but when it shut down the Hartleys had only one old swaybacked milk cow to sustain them, that and the galax, which earned a few nickels of barter at Mast's General Store. Jacob knew from the Sunday newspapers he bought that times were rough everywhere. Rich folks in New York had lost all their money and jumped out of buildings. Men rode boxcars town to town begging for work. But it was hard to believe any of them had less than Hartley and his family.

When Hartley saw Jacob he nodded but did not slow his pace. They were neither friends nor enemies, neighbors only in the sense that Jacob and Edna were the closest folks down the cove, though closest meant a half mile. Hartley had come up from Swain County eight years ago to work at the sawmill. The child had been a baby then, the wife seemingly decades younger than the cronish woman who walked beside the daughter. They would have passed without further acknowledgment except Edna came out on the porch.

"That hound of yours," she said to Hartley, "is it a egg-sucker?" Maybe she wasn't trying to be accusatory, but the words sounded so.

Hartley stopped in the road and turned toward the porch. Another man would have set the pokes down, but Hartley did not. He held them as if calculating their heft.

"What's the why of you asking that?" he said. The words were spoken in a tone that was neither angry nor defensive. It struck Jacob that even the man's voice had been worn down to a bare-boned flatness.

"Something's got in our henhouse and stole some," Edna said. "Just the eggs, so it ain't a fox nor weasel."

"So you reckon my dog."

Edna did not speak, and Hartley set the pokes down. He pulled a barlow knife from his tattered overalls. He softly called the hound and it sidled up to him. Hartley got down on one knee, closed his left hand on the scruff of the dog's neck as he settled the blade against its throat. The daughter and wife stood perfectly still, their faces blank as bread dough.

"I don't think it's your dog that's stealing the eggs," Jacob said.

"But you don't know for sure. It could be," Hartley said, the hound raising its head as Hartley's index finger rubbed the base of its skull.

Before Jacob could reply the blade whisked across the hound's windpipe. The dog didn't cry out or snarl. It merely sagged in Hartley's grip. Blood darkened the road.

"You'll know for sure now," Hartley said as he stood up. He lifted the dog by the scruff of the neck, walked over to the other side of the road and laid it in the weeds. "I'll get it on the way back this evening," he said, and picked up the pokes. Hartley began walking and his wife and daughter followed.

"Why'd you have to say something to him," Jacob said when the family had disappeared down the road. He stared at the place in the weeds where flies and yellow jackets began to gather.

"How'd I know he'd do such a thing?" Edna said.

"You know how proud a man he is."

Jacob let those words linger. In January when two feet of snow had shut nearly everyone in, Jacob had gone up the skid trail on horseback, a salted pork shoulder strapped to the saddle. "We could be needing that meat soon enough ourselves," Edna had said, but he'd gone anyway. When Jacob got to the cabin he'd found the family at the plank table eating. The wooden bowls before them held a thick liquid lumped with a few crumbs of fatback. The milk pail hanging over the fire was filled with the same gray-colored gruel. Jacob had set the pork shoulder on the table. The meat had a deep wood-smoke odor, and the woman and child swallowed every few seconds to conceal their salivating. "I ain't got no money to buy it," Hartley said. "So I'd appreciate you taking your meat and leaving." Jacob had left, but after closing the cabin door he'd laid the pork on the front stoop. The next morning Jacob had found the meat on his own doorstep.

Jacob gazed past Hartley's dog, across the road to the acre of corn where he'd work till suppertime. He hadn't hoed a single row yet but already felt tired all the way to his bones.

"I didn't want that dog killed," Edna said. "That wasn't my intending."

"Like it wasn't your intending for Joel and Mary to leave and never darken our door again," Jacob replied. "But it happened, didn't it."

He turned and walked to the woodshed to get his hoe.

The next morning the dog was gone from the roadside and more eggs were missing. It was Saturday, so Jacob rode the horse down to Boone, not just to get his newspaper but to talk to the older farmers who gathered at Mast's General Store. As he rode he remembered the morning six years ago when Joel dropped his bowl of oatmeal on the floor. Careless, but twelve-year-olds did careless things. It was part of being a child. Edna made the boy eat the oatmeal off the floor with his spoon. "Don't do it," Mary had told her younger brother, but he had, whimpering the whole time. Mary, who was sixteen, eloped two weeks later. "I'll never come back, not even to visit," a note left on the kitchen table said. Mary had been true to her word.

As Jacob rode into Boone, he saw the truck the savings and loan had repossessed from him parked by the courthouse. It was a vehicle made for hauling crops to town, bringing back salt blocks and fertilizer and barbed wire, but he'd figured no farmer could have afforded to buy it at auction. Maybe a store owner or county employee, he supposed, someone who still used a billfold instead of a change purse like the one he now took a nickel from after tying his horse to the hitching post. Jacob entered the store. He nodded at the older men, then laid his coin on the counter. Erwin Mast handed him last Sunday's *Raleigh News*.

"Don't reckon there's any letters?" Jacob asked.

"No, nothing this week," Erwin said, though he could have added, "or the last month or last year." Joel was in the navy, stationed somewhere in the Pacific. Mary lived with her husband and her own child on a farm in Haywood County, sixty miles away but it could have been California for all the contact Jacob and Edna had with her.

Jacob lingered by the counter. When the old men paused in their conversation, he told them about the eggs.

"And you're sure it ain't a dog?" Sterling Watts asked.

"Yes. There wasn't a bit of splatter or shell on the straw."

"Rats will eat a egg," Erwin offered from behind the counter.

"There'd still be something left, though," Bascombe Lindsey said.

"They's but one thing it can be," Sterling Watts said with finality.

"What's that," Jacob asked.

"A big yaller rat snake. They'll swallow two or three eggs whole and leave not a dribble of egg."

"I've heard such myself," Bascombe agreed. "Never seen it but heard of it."

"Well, one got in my henhouse," Sterling said. "And it took me near a month to figure out how to catch the damn thing."

"How did you?" Jacob asked.

"Went fishing," Sterling said.

That night Jacob hoed in his cornfield till dark. He ate his supper, then went to the woodshed and found a fishhook. He tied three yards of line to it and went to the henhouse. The bantam had one egg under her. Jacob took the egg and made as small a hole as possible with the barb. He slowly worked the whole hook into the egg, then tied the line to a nail head behind the nesting box. Three yards, Watson had said. That way the snake would swallow the whole egg before a tight line set the hook.

"I ain't about to go out there come morning and deal with no snake," Edna said when he told her what he'd done. She sat in the ladderback rocking chair, her legs draped by a quilt. He'd made the chair for her to sit in when she'd been pregnant with Joel. The wood was cherry, not the most practical for furniture, but he'd wanted it to be pretty.

"I'll deal with it," Jacob said.

For a few moments he watched her sew, the fine blue thread repairing the binding of the Bear's Claw quilt. Edna had worked since dawn, but she couldn't stop even now. Jacob sat down at the kitchen table and spread out the newspaper. On the front page Roosevelt said things were getting better, but the rest of the news argued otherwise. Strikers had been shot at a cotton mill. Men whose crime was hiding in boxcars to search for work had been beaten with clubs by lawmen and hired railroad goons.

"What you claimed this morning about me running off Joel and Mary," Edna said, her needle not pausing as she spoke, "that was a spiteful thing to say. Those kids never went hungry a day in their lives. Their clothes was patched and they had shoes and coats."

He knew he should let it go, but the image of Hartley's knife opening the hound's throat had snared in his mind.

"You could have been easier on them."

"The world's a hard place," Edna replied. "There was need for them to know that."

"They'd have learned soon enough on their own," Jacob said.

"They needed to be prepared, and I prepared them. They ain't in a hobo camp or barefoot like Hartley and his clan. If they can't be grateful for that, there's nothing I can do about it now."

"There's going to be better times," Jacob said. "This depression can't last forever, but the way you treated them will."

"It's lasted nine years," Edna said. "And I see no sign of it letting up. The price we're getting for corn and cabbage is the same. We're still living on half of what we did before."

She turned back to the quilt's worn binding and no other words were spoken between them. After a while Edna put down her sewing and went to bed. Jacob soon followed. Edna tensed as he settled his body beside hers.

"I don't want us to argue," Jacob said, and laid his hand on her shoulder. She flinched from his touch, moved farther away.

"You think I've got no feelings," Edna said, her face turned so she spoke at the wall. "Stingy and mean-hearted. But maybe if I hadn't been we'd not have anything left."

Despite his weariness, Jacob had trouble going to sleep. When he finally did, he dreamed of men hanging onto boxcars while other men beat them with sticks. Those beaten wore muddy brogans and overalls, and he knew they weren't laid-off mill workers or coal miners but farmers like himself.

Jacob woke in the dark. The window was open and before he could fall back asleep he heard something from inside the henhouse. He pulled on his overalls and boots, then went out on the porch and lit a lantern. The sky was thick with stars and a wet moon lightened the ground, but the windowless henhouse was pitch dark. It had crossed his mind that if a yellow rat snake could eat an egg a copperhead or satinback could as well, and he wanted to see where he stepped. He went to the wood-shed and got a hoe for the killing.

Jacob crossed the foot log and stepped up to the entrance. He held the lantern out and checked the nesting box. The bantam was in it, but no eggs lay under her. It took him a few moments to find the fishing line, leading toward the back corner like a single strand of a spider's web. He readied the hoe in his hand and took a step inside. He held the lamp before him and saw Hartley's daughter huddled in the corner, the line disappearing into her closed mouth.

She did not try to speak as he kneeled before her. Jacob set the hoe and lantern down and took out his pocketknife, then cut the line inches above where it disappeared between her lips. For a few moments he did nothing else.

"Let me see," he said, and though she did not open her mouth she did not resist as his fingers did so. He found the hook's barb sunk deep in her cheek and was relieved. He'd feared it would be in her tongue or, much worse, deep in her throat.

"We got to get that hook out," Jacob told her, but still she said nothing. Her eyes did not widen in fear and he wondered if maybe she was in shock. The barb was too deep to wiggle free. He'd have to push it the rest of the way through.

"This is going to hurt, but just for a second," he said, and let his index finger and thumb grip the hook where it began to curve. He worked deeper into the skin, his thumb and finger slickened by blood and saliva. The child whimpered. Finally the barb broke through. He wiggled the shank out, the line coming last like thread completing a stitch.

"It's out now," he told her.

For a few moments Jacob did not get up. He thought about what to do next. He could carry her back to Hartley's shack and explain what happened, but he remembered the dog. He looked at her cheek and there was no tear, only a tiny hole that bled little more than a briar scratch would. He studied the hook for signs of rust. There didn't seem to be, so at least he didn't have to worry about the girl getting lockjaw. But it could still get infected.

"Stay here," Jacob said and went to the woodshed. He found the bottle of turpentine and returned. He took his handkerchief and soaked it, then opened the child's mouth and dabbed the wound, did the same outside to the cheek.

"Okay," Jacob said. He reached out his hands and placed them under her armpits. She was so light it was like lifting a rag doll. The child stood before him now, and for the first time he saw that her right hand held something. He picked up the lantern and saw it was an egg and that it was unbroken. Jacob nodded at the egg.

"You don't ever take them home, do you," he said. "You eat them here, right?"

The child nodded.

"Go ahead and eat it then," Jacob said, "but you can't come back anymore. If you do, your daddy will know about it. You understand?"

"Yes," she whispered, the first word she'd spoken.

"Eat it, then."

The girl raised the egg to her lips. A thin line of blood trickled down her chin as she opened her mouth. The shell crackled as her teeth bit down.

"Go home now," he said when she'd swallowed the last bit of shell. "And don't come back. I'm going to put another hook in them eggs and this time there won't be no line on it. You'll swallow that hook and it'll tear your guts up."

Jacob watched her walk up the skid trail until the dark enveloped her, then sat on the stump that served as a chopping block. He blew out the lantern and waited, though for what he could not say. After a while the moon and stars faded. In the east, darkness lightened to the color of indigo glass. The first outlines of the corn stalks and their leaves were visible now, reaching up from the ground like shabbily dressed arms.

Jacob picked up the lantern and turpentine and went to the shed, then on to the house. Edna was getting dressed as he came into the bedroom. Her back was to him.

"It was a snake," he said.

Edna paused in her dressing and turned. Her hair was down and her face not yet hardened to face the day's demands and he glimpsed the younger, softer woman she'd been twenty years ago when they'd married.

"You kill it?" she asked.

"Yes."

Her lips tightened.

"I hope you didn't just throw it out by the henhouse. I don't want to smell that thing rotting when I'm gathering eggs."

"I threw it across the road."

He got in the bed. Edna's form and warmth lingered on the feather mattress.

"I'll get up in a few minutes," he told her.

Jacob closed his eyes but did not sleep. Instead, he imagined towns where hungry men hung on boxcars looking for work that couldn't be found, shacks where families lived who didn't even have one swaybacked milk cow. He imagined cities where blood stained the sidewalks beneath buildings tall as ridges. He tried to imagine a place worse than where he was.

BACK OF BEYOND

When Parson drove to his shop that morning, the sky was the color of lead. Flurries settled on the pickup's windshield, lingered a moment before expiring. A heavy snow tonight, the weatherman warned, and it looked to be certain, everything getting quiet and still, waiting. Even more snow in the higher mountains, enough to make many roads impassable. It would be a profitable day, because Parson knew they'd come to his pawnshop to barter before emptying every cold-remedy shelf in town. They would hit Wal-Mart first because it was cheapest, then the Rexall, and finally the town's three convenience stores, coming from every way-back cove and hollow in the county, because walls and windows couldn't conceal the smell of meth.

Parson pulled his jeep into the parking lot of the cinder-block building with PARSON'S BUY AND SELL hung over the door. One of the addicts had brought an electric portable sign last week, had it in his truck bed with a trash can filled with red plastic letters to stick on it. The man told Parson the sign would ensure that potential customers noticed the pawnshop. You found me easy enough, Parson had replied. His watch said eight forty and the sign in the window said nine to six Tuesday through Saturday, but a gray decade-old Ford Escort had already nosed up to the building. The back windshield was damaged, cracks spreading outward like a spiderweb. The gas cap a stuffed rag. A woman sat in the driver's seat. She could have been waiting ten minutes or ten hours.

Parson got out of his truck, unlocked the door, and cut off the alarm. He turned on the lights and walked around the counter, placed the loaded Smith & Wesson revolver on the shelf below the register. The copper bell above the sill tinkled.

The woman waited in the doorway, a wooden butter churn and dasher clutched in her arms. Parson had to hand it to them, they were getting more imaginative. Last week the electric sign and false teeth, the week before that four bicycle tires and a chiropractic table. Parson nodded for the woman to come on in. She set the churn and dasher on the table.

"It's a antique," the woman said. "I seen one like it on TV and the fellow said it was worth a hundred dollars."

When the woman spoke Parson glimpsed the stubbed brown ruin inside her mouth. He could see her face clearly now, sunken cheeks and eyes, skin pale and furrowed. He saw where the bones, impatient, poked at her cheeks and chin. The eyes glossy but alive, restless and needful.

"You better find that fellow then," Parson said. "A fool like that don't come around often."

"It was my great-grandma's," the woman said, nodding at the churn, "so it's near seventy-five years old." She paused. "I guess I could take fifty for it."

Parson looked the churn over, lifted the dasher and inspected it as well. An antiques dealer in Asheville might give him a hundred.

"Twenty dollars," Parson said.

"That man on TV said . . ."

"You told me," Parson interrupted. "Twenty dollars is what I'll pay."

The woman looked at the churn a few moments, then back at Parson.

"Okay," she said.

She took the cash and stuffed the bills in her jeans. She did not leave.

"What?" Parson asked.

The woman hesitated, then raised her hands and took off her high school ring. She handed it to him, and Parson inspected it. "Class of 2000," the ring said.

"'Ten," he said, laying the ring on her side of the glass counter.

She didn't try to barter this time but instead slid the ring across the glass as if it were a piece in a board game. She held her fingers on the metal a few moments before letting go and holding out her palm.

By noon he'd had twenty customers and almost all were meth addicts. Parson didn't need to look at them to know. The odor of it came in the door with them, in their hair, their clothes, a sour ammonia smell like cat piss. Snow fell steady now and his business began slacking off, even the manic needs of the addicted deferring to the weather. Parson was finishing his lunch in the back room when the bell sounded again. He came out and found Sheriff Hawkins waiting at the counter.

"So what they stole now, Doug?" Parson asked.

"Couldn't it be I just come by to see my old high school buddy?"

Parson placed his hands on the counter.

"It could be, but I got the feeling it isn't."

"No," Hawkins said, smiling wryly. "In these troubled times there's not much chance to visit with friends and kin."

"Troubled times," Parson said. "But good for business, not just my business but yours."

"I guess that's a way of looking at it, though for me it's been too good of late."

Hawkins took a quick inventory of the bicycles and lawn mowers and chain saws filling the room's corners. Then he looked the room over again, more purposeful this time, checking behind the counter as well. The sheriff's brown eyes settled on the floor, where a shotgun lay amid other items yet to be tagged.

"That .410 may be what I'm looking for," the sheriff said. "Who brought it in?"

"Danny."

Parson handed the gun to the lawman without saying anything else.

Hawkins held the shotgun and studied the stock a moment.

"My eyes ain't what they used to be, Parson, but I'd say them initials carved in it are SJ, not DP."

"That gun Steve Jackson's?"

"Yes, sir," the sheriff replied, laying the shotgun on the counter. "Danny took it out of Steve's truck yesterday. At least that's what Steve believed."

"I didn't notice the initials," Parson said. "I figured it came off the farm."

Hawkins picked the shotgun off the counter and held it in one hand, studying it critically. He shifted it slightly, let his thumb rub the stock's varnished wood.

"I think I can talk Steve out of pressing charges."

"Don't do that as a favor to me," Parson said. "If his own daddy don't give a damn he's a thief, why should I?"

"How come you to think Ray doesn't care?" Hawkins asked.

"Because Danny's been bringing things to me from the farm for months. Ray knows where they're going. I called him three months ago and told him myself. He said he couldn't do anything about it."

"Doesn't look to be you're doing much about it either," the sheriff said. "I mean, you're buying from him, right?"

"If I don't he'll just drive down to Sylva and sell it there."

Parson looked out at the snow, the parking lot empty but for his and Hawkins's vehicles. He wondered if any customers had decided not to pull in because of the sheriff's car.

"You just as well go ahead and arrest him," Parson added. "You've seen enough of these meth addicts to know he'll steal something else soon enough."

"I didn't know he was on meth," Hawkins said.

"That's your job, isn't it," Parson replied, "to know such things?"

"There's too many of them to keep up with. This meth, it ain't like other drugs. Even cocaine and crack, at least those were expensive and hard to get. But this stuff, it's too easy." The sheriff looked out the window. "This snow's going to make for a long day, so I'd better get to it."

"So you're not going to arrest him?"

"No," Hawkins said. "He'll have to wait his turn. There's two dozen in line ahead of him. But you could do me a favor by giving him a call. Tell him this is his one chance, that next time I'll lock his ass up." Hawkins pressed his lips together a moment, pensive. "Hell, he might even believe it."

"I'll tell him," Parson said, "but I'll do it in person."

Parson went to the window and watched as the sheriff backed out onto the two-lane and drove toward the town's main drag. Snow stuck to the asphalt now, the jeep blanketed white. He'd watched Danny drive away the day before, the tailgate down and truck bed empty. Parson had known the truck bed would probably be empty when Danny headed out of town, no filled grocery bags or kerosene cans, because the boy lived in a world where food and warmth and clothing were no longer important. The only essentials were the red-and-white packs of Sudafed in the passenger's seat as the truck disappeared back into the folds of the higher mountains, headed up into Chestnut Cove, what Parson's father had called the back of beyond, the place where Parson and Ray had grown up.

He placed the pistol in his coat pocket and changed the OPEN sign to CLOSED. Once on the road, Parson saw the snow was dry, powdery, which would make the drive easier. He headed west and did not turn on the radio.

Except for two years in the army, Ray had lived his whole life in Chestnut Cove. He'd used his army pay to buy a farm adjacent to the one he'd grown up on and had soon after married Martha. Parson had joined the army as well but afterward went to Tuckasegee to live. When their parents had gotten too old to mend fences and feed livestock, plant and harvest the tobacco, Ray and Martha did it. Ray had never asked Parson to help, never expected him to, since he was twenty miles away in town. For his part, Parson had not been bitter when the farm was willed to the firstborn. Ray and Martha had earned it. By then Parson owned the pawnshop outright from the bank, had money enough. Ray and Martha sold their house and moved into the farmhouse, raised Danny and his three older sisters there.

Parson slowed as the road began a long curve around Brushy Mountain. The road soon forked and he went left. Another left and he was on a county road, poorly maintained because no wealthy Floridians had second homes on it. No guardrails. He met no other vehicle, because only a few people lived in the cove, had ever lived up here.

Parson parked beside Ray's truck and got out, stood a few moments before the homestead. He hadn't been up in nearly a year and supposed he should feel more than the burn of anger directed at his nephew. Some kind of nostalgia. But Parson couldn't summon it, and if he had, then what for? Working his ass off in August tobacco fields, milking cows on mornings so cold his hands numbed—the very things that had driven him away in the first place. Except for a thin ribbon of smoke unfurling from the chimney, the farm appeared forsaken. No cattle huddled against the snow, no TV or radio playing in the front room or kitchen. Parson had never regretted leaving, and never more so than now as his gaze moved from the rusting tractor and bailer to the sagging fences that held nothing in, settled on the shambling farmhouse itself, then turned toward the land between the barn and house.

Danny's battered blue-and-white trailer squatted in the pasture. Parson's feet made a whispery sound as he went to deal with his nephew before talking to his brother and sister-in-law. No footprints marked the snow between house and trailer. Parson knocked on the flimsy aluminum door and when no one answered went in. No lights were on and Parson wasn't surprised when he flipped a switch and nothing happened. His eyes slowly adjusted to the room's darkness, and he saw the card table, on it cereal boxes, some open, some not, a half-gallon milk container, its contents frozen solid. The room's busted-out window helped explain why. Two bowls scabbed with dried cereal lay on the table as well. Two spoons. Parson made his way to the back room, seeing first the kerosene heater beside the bed, the wire wick's muted orange glow. Two closely lumped mounds rose under a pile of quilts. *Like they're already laid out in their graves*, Parson thought as he leaned over and poked the bigger form.

"Get up, boy," Parson said.

But it was Ray's face and torso that emerged, swaddled in an array of shirts and sweaters. Martha's face appeared as well. They seemed like timid animals disturbed in their dens. For a few moments Parson could only stare at them. After decades in the most cynical of professions, he was amazed that anything could still stun him.

"Why in the hell aren't you in the house?" Parson asked finally.

It was Martha who replied.

"Danny, he's in there, sometimes his friends too." She paused. "It's just better, easier, if we're out here."

Parson looked at his brother. Ray was sixty-five years

old but he looked eighty, his mouth sunk in, skinny and feeble. His sister-in-law appeared a little better off, perhaps because she was a large, big-boned woman. But they both looked bad—hungry, weary, sickly. And scared. Parson couldn't remember his brother ever being scared, but he clearly was. Ray's right hand clutched a quilt end, and the hand was trembling. Parson and his wife, DeAnne, had divorced before they'd had children. A blessing, he now saw, because it prevented any possibility of ending up like this.

Martha had not been above lording her family over Parson in the past, enough to where he'd made his visits rare and short. You missed out not having any kids, she'd said to him more than once, words he'd recalled times when Danny pawned a chain saw or posthole digger or some other piece of the farm. It said much of how beaten down Martha appeared that Parson mustered no pleasure in recalling her words now.

He settled his eyes on the kerosene heater emitting its feeble warmth.

"Yeah, it looks to be easier out here all right," he said.

Ray licked his cracked lips and then spoke, his voice raspy.

"That stuff, whatever you call it, has done made my boy crazy. He don't know nothing but a craving."

"It ain't his fault, it's the craving," Martha added,

sitting up enough to reveal that she too wore layers of clothing. "Maybe I done something wrong raising him, petted him too much since he was my only boy. The girls always claimed I favored him."

"The girls been up here?" Parson asked. "Seen you like this?"

Martha shook her head.

"They got their own families to look after," she said.

Ray's lower lip trembled.

"That ain't it. They're scared to come up here."

Parson looked at his brother. He had thought this was going to be so much easier, a matter of twenty dollars, that and relaying the sheriff's threat.

"How long you been out here, Ray?"

"I ain't sure," Ray replied.

Martha spoke.

"Not more than a week."

"How long has the electricity been off?"

"Since October," Ray said.

"Is all you've had to eat on that table?"

Ray and Martha didn't meet his eyes.

A family photograph hung on the wall. Parson wondered when it had been put up, before or after Danny moved out. Danny was sixteen, maybe seventeen in the photo. Cocksure but also petulant, the expression of a young man who'd been indulged all his life. His family's golden child. Parson suddenly realized something.

"He's cashing your Social Security checks, isn't he?"

"It ain't his fault," Martha said.

Parson still stood at the foot of the bed, Ray and Martha showing no indication of getting out. They looked like children waiting for him to turn out the light and leave so they could go to sleep. Pawnbrokers, like emergency room doctors and other small gods, had to abjure sympathy. That had never been a problem for Parson. As DeAnne had told him several times, he was a man incapable of understanding another person's heart. You can't feel love, Parson, she'd said. It's like you were given a shot years ago and inoculated.

"I'll get your electricity turned back on," Parson told his brother. "Can you still drive?"

"I can drive," Ray said. "Only thing is, Danny uses that truck for his doings."

"That's going to change," Parson said.

"It ain't Danny's fault," Martha said again.

"Enough of it is," Parson replied.

He went to the corner and lifted the kerosene can. Half full.

"What you taking our kerosene for?" Martha asked.

Parson didn't reply. He left the trailer and trudged back through the snow, the can heavy and awkward, his breath quick white heaves. Not so different from those mornings he'd carried a gallon pail of warm milk from barn to house. Even as a child he'd wanted to leave this place. Never loved it the way Ray had. *Inoculated*.

Parson set the can on the lowered tailgate and perched himself on it as well. He took the lighter and cigarettes from his coat pocket and stared at the house while he smoked. Kindling and logs brought from the woodshed littered the porch. No attempt had been made to stack it.

It would be easy to do, Parson told himself. No one had stirred when he'd driven up and parked five yards from the front door. No one had even peeked out a window. He could step up on the porch and soak the logs and kindling with kerosene, then go around back and pour the rest on the back door. Then Hawkins would put it down as just another meth explosion caused by some punk who couldn't pass high school chemistry. And if others were in there, they were people quite willing to scare two old folks out of their home. No worse than setting fire to a woodpile infested with copperheads. Parson finished his cigarette and flicked it toward the house, a quick hiss as snow quenched the smoldering butt.

He eased off the tailgate and stepped onto the porch, tried the doorknob, and when it turned, stepped into the front room. A dying fire glowed in the hearth. The room had been stripped of anything that could be sold, the only furnishing left a couch pulled up by the fireplace. Even wallpaper had been torn off a wall. The odor of meth infiltrated everything, coated the walls and floor.

Danny and a girl Parson didn't know lay on the couch, a quilt thrown over them. Their clothes were worn and dirty and smelled as if lifted from a Dumpster. As Parson moved toward the couch he stepped over rotting sandwich scraps in paper sacks, candy wrappers, spills from soft drinks. If human shit had been on the floor he would not have been surprised.

"Who is he?" the girl asked Danny.

"A man who's owed twenty dollars," Parson said.

Danny sat up slowly, the girl as well, black stringy hair, flesh whittled away by the meth. Parson looked for something that might set her apart from the dozen or so similar women he saw each week. It took a few moments but he found one thing, a blue four-leaf clover tattooed on her forearm. Parson looked into her dead eyes and saw no indication luck had found her.

"Got tired of stealing from your parents, did you?" Parson asked his nephew.

"What are you talking about?" Danny said.

His eyes were light blue, similar to the girl's eyes, bright but at the same time dead. A memory of elementary school came to Parson of colorful insects pinned and enclosed beneath glass.

"That shotgun you stole."

Danny smiled but kept his mouth closed. *Some vanity still left in him*, Parson mused, remembering how the boy had preened even as a child, a comb at the ready in his shirt pocket, nice clothes.

"I didn't figure him to miss it much," Danny said. "That gas station he owns does good enough business for him to buy another."

"You're damn lucky it's me telling you and not the sheriff, though he'll be up here soon as the roads are clear."

Danny looked at the dying fire as if he spoke to it, not Parson.

"So why did you show up? I know it's not to warn me Hawkins is coming."

"Because I want my twenty dollars," Parson said.

"I don't have your twenty dollars," Danny said.

"Then you're going to pay me another way."

"And what's that?"

"By getting in the truck," Parson said. "I'm taking your sorry ass to the bus station. One-way ticket to Atlanta."

"What if I don't want to do that?" Danny said.

There had been a time the boy could have made that comment formidable, for he'd been broad-shouldered and stout, an all-county tight end, but he'd shucked off fifty pounds, the muscles melted away same as his teeth. Parson didn't even bother showing him the revolver.

"Well, you can wait here until the sheriff comes and hauls your worthless ass off to jail."

Danny stared at the fire. The girl reached out her hand, let it settle on Danny's forearm. The room was utterly quiet except for a few crackles and pops from the fire. No time ticked on the fireboard. Parson had bought the Franklin clock from Danny two months ago. He'd thought briefly of keeping it himself but had resold it to the antiques dealer in Asheville.

"If I get arrested then it's an embarrassment to you. Is that the reason?" Danny asked.

"The reason for what?" Parson replied.

"That you're acting like you give a damn about me."

Parson didn't answer, and for almost a full minute no one spoke. It was the girl who finally broke the silence.

"What about me?"

"I'll buy you a ticket or let you out in Asheville," Parson said. "But you're not staying here."

"We can't go nowhere without our drugs," the girl said.

"Get them then."

She went into the kitchen and came back with a brown paper bag, its top half folded over and crumpled.

"Hey," she said when Parson took it from her.

"I'll give it back when you're boarding the bus," he said.

Danny looked to be contemplating something and Parson wondered if he might have a knife on him, possibly a revolver of his own, but when Danny stood up, hands empty, no handle jutted from his pocket.

"Get your coats on," Parson said. "You'll be riding in the back."

"It's too cold," the girl said.

"No colder than that trailer," Parson said.

Danny paused as he put on a denim jacket.

"So you went out there first."

"Yes," Parson said.

A few moments passed before Danny spoke.

"I didn't make them go out there. They got scared by some guys that were here last week." Danny sneered then, something Parson suspected the boy had probably practiced in front of mirror. "I check on them more than you do," he said.

"Let's go," Parson said. He dangled the paper bag in front of Danny and the girl, then took the revolver out of his pocket. "I've got both of these, just in case you think you might try something."

They went outside. The snow still fell hard, the way back down to the county road now only a white absence of trees. Danny and the girl stood by the truck's tailgate, but they didn't get in. Danny nodded at the paper bag in Parson's left hand.

"At least give us some so we can stand the cold."

Parson opened the bag, took out one of the baggies. He had no idea if one was enough for the both of them or not. He threw the packet into the truck bed and watched Danny and the girl climb in after it. *No different than you'd do for two hounds with a dog biscuit*, Parson thought, shoving the kerosene can farther inside and hitching the tailgate.

He got in the truck and cranked the engine, drove slowly down the drive. Once on the county road he turned left and began the fifteen-mile trip to Sylva. Danny and the girl huddled against the back window, their heads and Parson's separated by a quarter inch of glass. Their proximity made the cab feel claustrophobic, especially when he heard the girl's muffled crying. Parson turned on the radio, the one station he could pick up promising a foot of snow by nightfall. Then a song he hadn't heard in thirty years, Ernest Tubb's "Walking the Floor Over You." Halfway down Brushy Mountain the road made a quick veer and plunge. Danny and the girl slid across the bed and banged against the tailgate. A few moments later, when the road leveled out, Danny pounded the window with his fist, but Parson didn't look back. He just turned up the radio.

At the bus station, Danny and the girl sat on a bench while Parson bought the tickets. The Atlanta bus wasn't due for an hour so Parson waited across the room from them. The girl had a busted lip, probably from sliding into the tailgate. She dabbed her mouth with a Kleenex, then stared a long time at the blood on the tissue. Danny was agitated, hands restless, constantly shifting on the bench as though unable to find a comfortable position. He finally got up and came over to where Parson sat, stood before him.

"You never liked me, did you?" Danny said.

Parson looked up at the boy, for though in his twenties Danny was still a boy, would die a boy, Parson believed.

"No, I guess not," Parson said.

"What's happened to me," Danny said. "It ain't all my fault."

"I keep hearing that."

"There's no good jobs in this county. You can't make a living farming no more. If there'd been something for me, a good job I mean."

"I hear there's lots of jobs in Atlanta," Parson said. "It's booming down there, so you're headed to the land of no excuses."

"I don't want to go down there." Danny paused. "I'll die there."

"What you're using will kill you here same as Atlanta. At least down there you won't take your momma and daddy with you."

"You've never cared much for them before, especially Momma. How come you to care now?"

Parson thought about the question, mulled over several possible answers.

"I guess because no one else does," he finally said.

When the bus came, Parson walked with them to the loading platform. He gave the girl the bag and the tickets, then watched the bus groan out from under the awning and head south. There would be several stops before Atlanta, but Danny and the girl would stay aboard because of a promised two hundred dollars sent via Western Union. A promise Parson would not keep.

The Winn-Dixie shelves were emptied of milk and bread but enough of all else remained to fill four grocery bags. Parson stopped at Steve Jackson's gas station and filled the kerosene can. Neither man mentioned the shotgun now reracked against the pickup's back window. The trip back to Chestnut Cove was slower, more snow on the roads, the visibility less as what dim light the day had left drained into the high mountains to the west. Dark by five, he knew, and it was already past four. After the truck slid a second time, spun, and stopped precariously close to a drop-off, Parson stayed in first or second gear. A trip of thirty minutes in good weather took him an hour.

When he got to the farmhouse, Parson took a flashlight from the dash, carried the groceries into the kitchen. He brought the kerosene into the farmhouse as well, then walked down to the trailer and went inside.

The heater's metal wick still glowed orange. Parson cut it off so the metal would cool.

He shone the light on the bed. They were huddled together, Martha's head tucked under Ray's chin, his arms enclosing hers. They were asleep and seemed at peace. Parson felt regret in waking them and for a few minutes did not. He brought a chair from the front room and placed it by the foot of the bed. He waited. Martha woke first. The room was dark and shadowy but she sensed his presence, turned and looked at him. She shifted to see him better and Ray's eyes opened as well.

"You can go back to the house now," Parson said.

They only stared back at him.

"He's gone," Parson said. "And he won't come back. There will be no reason for his friends to come either."

Martha stirred now, sat up in the bed.

"What did you do to him?"

"I didn't do anything," Parson said. "He and his girlfriend wanted to go to Atlanta and I drove them to the bus station."

Martha didn't look like she believed him. She got slowly out of the bed and Ray did as well. They put on their shoes, then moved tentatively to the trailer's door, seemingly with little pleasure. They hesitated.

"Go on," Parson said. "I'll bring the heater."

Parson went and got the kerosene heater. He stooped and lifted it slowly, careful to use his legs instead of his back. Little fuel remained in it, so it wasn't heavy, just awkward. When he came into the front room, his brother and sister-in-law still stood inside the door.

"Hold the door open," he told Ray, "so I can get this thing outside."

Parson got the heater down the steps and carried it the rest of the way. Once inside the farmhouse he set it near the hearth, filled the tank, and turned it on. He and Ray gathered logs and kindling off the front porch and got a good flame going in the fireplace. The flue wasn't drawing as it should. By the time Parson had adjusted it a smoky odor filled the room, but that was a better smell than the meth. The three of them sat on the couch and unwrapped the sandwiches. They did not speak even when they'd finished, just stared at the hearth as flame shadows trembled on the walls. Parson thought what an old human feeling this must be, how ten thousand years ago people would have done the same thing on a cold night, would have eaten, then settled before the fire, looked into it and found peace, knowing they'd survived the day and now could rest.

Martha began snoring softly and Parson grew sleepy as well. He roused himself, looked over at his brother, whose eyes still watched the fire. Ray didn't look sleepy, just lost in thought.

Parson got up and stood before the hearth, let the heat soak into his clothes and skin before going out into the cold. He took the revolver from his pocket and gave it to Ray.

"In case any of Danny's friends give you any trouble," Parson said. "I'll get your power turned back on in the morning."

Martha awoke with a start. For a few moments she seemed not to know where she was.

"You ain't thinking of driving back to Tuckasegee tonight?" Ray asked. "The roads will be dangerous."

"I'll be all right. My jeep can handle them."

"I still wish you wouldn't go," Ray said. "You ain't slept under this roof for near forty years. That's too long."

"Not tonight," Parson said.

Ray shook his head.

"I never thought things could ever get like this," he said. "The world, I just don't understand it no more."

Martha spoke.

"Did Danny say where he'd be staying?"

"No," Parson said, and turned to leave.

"I'd rather be in that trailer tonight and knowing he was in this house. Knowing where he is, if he's alive or dead," she said as Parson reached for the doorknob. "You had no right."

Parson walked out to the jeep. It took a few tries but the engine turned over and he made his way down the drive. Only flurries glanced the windshield now. Parson drove slowly and several times had to stop and get out to find the road among the white blankness. Once out of Chestnut Cove, he made better time, but it was after midnight when he got back to Tuckasegee. His alarm clock was set for seven thirty. Parson reset it for eight thirty. If he was late opening, a few minutes or even an hour, it wouldn't matter. Whatever time he showed up, they'd still be there.

DEAD CONFEDERATES

I never cared for Wesley Davidson when he was alive and seeing him beside me laid out dead didn't much change that. Knowing a man for years and feeling hardly anything in his passing might make you think poorly of me, but the hard truth is had you known Wesley you'd probably feel the same. You might do what I done—shovel dirt on him with not so much as a mumble of a prayer. Bury him under a tombstone with another man's name on it, another man's birth and dying day chipped in the marble, me and an old man all of the living ever to know that was where Wesley Davidson laid in the ground.

"I've a notion you're needing some extra money," Wesley says two weeks earlier at work, which isn't a big secret since the whole road crew's in the DOT parking lot that afternoon when the bank man comes by to chat about my overdrawn account, saying he's sorry my momma's in the hospital with no insurance but if I don't get him some money soon he'll be taking my truck. Soon as the bank man leaves Wesley saunters up to me.

I act like I haven't heard him, because like I said I never cared much for Wesley. He's a big talker but little else, always shucking his work off on the rest of us. A stout man, six foot tall and three hundred easy, a big old sow belly that sways side to side when he takes a notion to work. But that's a sight you seldom see, because he mainly leans on a shovel or lays in the shade asleep. His uncle's the road crew boss, and he lets Wesley do about what he wants, including come in late, the rest of us all clocked in and ready to pull out while Wesley's Ford Ranger is pulling in, a big rebel flag decal covering the back window. Wesley's always been big into that Confederate stuff, wearing a CSA belt buckle, rebel flag tattoo on his arm. He wears a gray CSA cap too, wears it on the job. There's no black guys on our crew, only a handful in the whole county, but you're still not supposed to wear that kind of thing. But with his uncle running the show Wesley gets away with it.

"You want to make some easy money or not?" he

says to me later at our lunch break. He grunts and sits down in the shade beside me while I get my sandwich and apple from my lunch box. Wesley's got three Hardee's sausage biscuits in a bag and scarfs them down in about thirty seconds, then lights a cigarette. I don't smoke myself and don't cotton much to the smelling of it when I'm eating. I could tell him so, could tell him I like eating my lunch alone if he'd not noticed, but getting on Wesley's bad side would just get me on my boss's bad side as well. It's more than just that, though. I'm willing to listen to anyone who could help me get some money.

"What you got in mind?" I say.

He points to his CSA belt buckle.

"You know what one of them's worth, a real one?"

"No," I say, though I figure maybe fifty or a hundred dollars.

Wesley pulls out two wadded-up catalog pages from his back pocket.

"Look here," he says and points at a picture of a belt buckle and the number below it. "Eighteen hundred dollars," he says and moves his finger down the paper. "Twenty-four hundred. Twelve hundred. Four thousand." He holds his finger there for a few seconds. "Four thousand," saying it again. He shoves the other page in my face. It's filled with buttons that fetch two hundred to a thousand dollars apiece.

"I'd of not thought they'd bring that much," I say.

"I'll not even tell you what a sword brings. You'd piss your pants if I did."

"So what's that have to do with me getting some money?"

"Cause I know where we can find such things as this," Wesley says, shaking the paper at me. "Find them where they ain't been all rusted up so's they'll be all the more pricey. You help and you get twenty-five percent."

And what I figure is some DOT bulldozer has rooted something up. Maybe some place where soldiers camped or done some fighting. I'm figuring it's some kind of flimflam, like he wants me to help buy a metal detector or something with what little money I got left. He must take me for one dumb hillbilly to go along with such a scheme and I tell him as much.

He just grins at me, the kind of grin that argues I don't know very much.

"You got a shovel and pickax?" he asks. "Or did the bank repo them as well?"

"I got a shovel and a pickax," I say. "I know how to do more than lean on them too."

He knows my meaning but just laughs, tells me what he's got his mind scheming over. I start to say there's no way in hell I'm doing such a thing but he puts his hand out like stopping traffic, tells me not to yes or no him until I've had time to sift it over good in my mind.

"I ain't hearing a word till tomorrow," he says. "Think about how a thousand dollars, maybe more, could put some padding in that wallet. Think about what that money can do for your momma."

He says the words about Momma last for he knows that notion will hang heavy on me if nothing else does.

I go by the hospital on the way home. They let me see her for a few minutes, and afterward the nurse says she'll be able to go home in three days.

"She's got a lot of life in her yet," the nurse tells me in the hallway.

That's good news, better than I expected. I go down to the billing office and the news there isn't so good. Though I've already paid three thousand I'll be owing another four by the time she gets out. I go back to my trailer and there's no way I can't help pondering about that money Wesley's big-talking about. I think about how Daddy worked himself to death before he was sixty and Momma hanging on long enough to be taught that fifty years of working first light to bedtime can't get you enough ahead to afford an operation and a two-week stay in a hospital. I'm pondering where's the fair in that when there's men who do no more than hit a ball good or throw one through a hoop and they live in mansions and could *buy* themselves a hospital if they was to need one. I think of the big houses built up at Wolf Laurel by doctors and bankers from Charlotte and Raleigh. Second homes, they call them, though some cost a million dollars. You could argue they worked hard for those homes, but no harder than Momma and Daddy worked.

By dawn I know certain I'm going to do it. When I say as much to Wesley at our morning break he smiles.

"Figured you would," he says.

"When?" I ask.

"Night, of course," he says, "a clear night when the moon is waxed up full. That way we'll not give ourselves away with a flashlight."

And him thinking it out enough to use moonlight gives me some confidence in him, makes me think it could work. Because that's the other thing bothering me besides the right and the wrong of it. If we get caught we'd be for sure doing some jailhouse time.

"I done thought this thing out from ever which angle," Wesley says. "I been scouting the cemeteries here to Flag Pond, looking for the right sort of graves, them that belongs to officers. I'm figuring the higher the rank the likelier to be booty there, maybe even a sword. Finally found me a couple of lieutenants. Never reckoned to find a general. From what I read most all them that did the generaling was Virginians. Found Yankee soldiers in them graveyards as well, including a captain."

"A captain outranks a lieutenant, don't he?" I ask.

"Yeah, but them that buys this stuff pay double if it's Confederate."

"And you can sell it easy?" I say. "I mean you don't have to fence it or anything like that?"

"Hell, no. They got these big sellings and swappings all over the place. Got one in Asheville next month. You show them what you got and they'll open their billfolds and fling that money at you."

He shuts up for a moment then, because he's starting to realize how easy it all sounds, and how much money I might start figuring to be my share. He lays his big yellow front teeth out on his lower lip, worrying his mind to figure a way to take back some of what he just said.

"Course they ain't going to pay near the price I showed you on them sheets. We'll be lucky to get half that."

I know that for a lie before it's left Wesley's lips, but I don't say anything, just know that I'll damn well be there with him when he sells what we find.

"What do we do next?" I say.

"Just wait for a clear night and a big old harvest moon," Wesley says, looking up at the sky like he might be expecting one to show up any minute. "That and keep your mouth shut about it. I've not told another person about this and I want it to stay that way."

Wait is what we do for two weeks, because that first night I look up from my yard the moon's all skinny and looks to be no more than something you might hang a coat on. Every night I watch the moon filling itself up like a big bowl, scooting the shadows out in the field back closer to the trees. Momma's back home and doing good, back to where she's looking more to be her ownself again. The folks at the hospital say she'll be eligible for the Medicaid come January and that's all for the good. That means I can go with Wesley just this one time, pay off that hospital bill, and be done with it.

Finally the right night comes, the moon full and leaning down close to the world. A hunter's moon, my daddy used to call it, and easy enough to see why, for such a moon makes tramping through woods a lot easier.

Tramping through a graveyard as well, for come ten o'clock that's what we're doing. We've hid his truck down past the entrance, a few yards back in a turn-around where, at least at night, no one would likely see it. We don't walk through the gate because that's where the caretaker's shack is. Instead we follow the fence up a hill through some trees, a pickax and shovel in my hands and nothing in Wesley's but a plastic garbage bag. It's late October and the air has that rinsed-clean feel. There's leaves that have fallen and acorns and they crackle under my feet, each one sounding loud as a .22 to me. I catch a whiff of a woodstove and find the glow of the porch light.

"You ain't worried none about that caretaker?" I say.

"Hell no. He's near eighty years old. He's probably been asleep since seven o'clock."

"He'd not have a fire going if he was asleep."

"That old man ain't going to bother us none," Wesley says, saying it like just his saying so makes it final.

We're soon moving amongst the stones, the moon brighter now that we're in the open. Its light lays down all silvery on the granite and marble, on the ground itself. It's quieter here, no more acorns and leaves, just cushiony grass like on a golf course. But it's too quiet, in a spooky kind of way. Because you know folks are here, hundreds of them, and not a one will say ever a word more on this earth. The only sound is Wesley's breathing and grunting. We've walked no more than a half mile and he's already laboring. A car comes up the road, headlights sweeping over a few tombstones as it takes the curve. It doesn't slow down but heads on toward Marshall.

"I got to catch my breath," Wesley says, and we stop a minute. We're on a ridge now, and I can see a whole passel of stars spilled out over the sky. As clear a night as you can get, and I reckon it's easy enough for God to see me from up there. That thought bothers me some, but it's a lot easier to have a conscience about something if you figure it all the way right or all the way wrong. Doing what we're doing is a sin for sure, but not taking care of the woman who birthed and raised you is a worse one. That's what I tell myself anyway.

"It's not much farther," Wesley says, saying it more for his own benefit than for me. He shakes his shoulders like a plow horse getting the trace chains more comfortable and walks down the yonder side of the hill until he comes to where a little Confederate flag is planted by a marble tombstone.

"Kind of them Daughters of the Confederacy biddies to sight-map the spot for us," Wesley says.

He pulls up the flag and throws it behind the stone like it was no more than a weed. He flicks his cigarette lighter and says the words out loud like I can't read them for myself.

"Lieutenant Gerald Ross Witherspoon. North Carolina Twenty-fifth. Born November 12, 1820. Died January 20, 1890."

"Dug up October 23, 2007," Wesley adds, and gives a good snort. He lights a cigarette and sets himself down by the grave. "You best get to it. We got all night but not an hour more."

"What about you?" I say. "I ain't doing all this digging alone."

"We'd just get in the other's way doing it as a team," Wesley says, then takes a big suck on his cigarette. "Don't fret, son. I'll spell you directly."

I lift my pickax and go to it. Yesterday's rain had

left some sog and squish in the ground so the first dirt breaks easy as wet sawdust. I get the shovel and scoop what I've loosed on the grass.

"People will know it's been dug," I say, pausing to gain back my breath.

And that's a new thought for me, because somehow up to now I'd had it figured if they didn't catch us in the graveyard we'd be home free. But two big holes are bound to have the law looking for those that dug them.

"And we'll be long gone when they do," Wesley says.

"You're not worried about it?" I say, because all of a sudden I am. Somebody could see the truck coming or going. We could drop something and in the dark not even know we'd left it behind.

"No," Wesley says. "The law will figure it for some of them voodoo devil worshippers. They'll not think to trouble upstanding citizens like us about it."

Wesley flares his lighter and lights another cigarette.

"We best get back to it," he says, nodding at the pickax in my hand.

"Don't seem to be no we to it," I say.

"Like I said, I'll spell you directly."

But directly turns out to be a long time. When I'm up to my chest I know I'm a good four feet down and he still hasn't got off his ass. I'm pouring sweat and raising crop rows of blisters on my palms. I'm about to tell

Wesley that I've dug four feet and he can at least dig two when the pickax strikes wood. A big splinter of it comes up, and it's cedar, which I always heard was the least likely wood to rot. I ponder a few moments why that grave's not a full six foot deep and then remember the date on the stone. Late January the ground would have been hard as iron. It would have been easy to figure four foot would do the job well enough.

"Hit it," I say.

Wesley gets up then.

"Dig some around it so we got room to get it open."

I do what he tells me, clearing a good foot to one side.

"I'll take over for you," he says, and crawls into the hole with me. "Probably be easier if you was to get out," he adds, picking up the shovel, but I ain't about to because I wouldn't put it past him to slip whatever he finds into his pocket.

"I wouldn't be one to try and hide something from you," Wesley says, which only tells me that's exactly what he was pondering.

We wedge ourselves sideways like we're on a cliff edge to get off the coffin. Then Wesley takes the shovel and pries open the lid.

The moon can't settle its light into the hole as easy as on level ground so it's hard to see clear at first. There's

a silk shirt you can tell even now was white and a belt
and its buckle and some moldy old shoes, but what once
filled the shoes and shirt looks to be little more than
the wind that blusters a shirt on a clothesline. Wesley
lifts the garment with his shovel tip and some dust and
bones the color of dried bamboo spill out. He throws
his shovel out of the hole and flicks his lighter. Wesley
holds the lighter close to the belt buckle. There's rust on
it, but you can make out C S stamped on the metal, not
CSA. Wesley lifts the buckle and pulls off what little is
left of the belt.

"It's a good one," he says, "but not near the best."

"How much you reckon it's worth?"

"A thousand at most," Wesley says after giving it a
good eyeballing.

I figure the real price to be double that, but I'll be
there when the bartering gets done so there's no need
to argue now. Wesley grunts and gets on his knees to
sift through the shirt, even checking inside what's left
of the shoes.

"Ain't nothing else," he says, and stands up.

I lift myself from the hole but it's not as easy for
Wesley. Though the hole's only four foot he's not able
to haul himself out. He gets halfway then slides back,
panting like a hound.

"I'll need your hand," he says. "I ain't no string bean
like you."

I give him a tug and Wesley wallows out, dirt crumbs all over his shirt and pants. He puts the buckle in the pillow sheet and knots it.

"The other one's down that way," Wesley says, and nods toward the caretaker's shack. He slides up his sleeve and checks his watch. "One fifteen. We making good time," he says.

We start down the hill, weaving our way through the stones laid out like a maze. Then a cloud smudges the moon and there's not enough light from the stars to see our own feet. We stop and I have a worrisome thought of something holding that cloud there the rest of the night, me and Wesley bumping into stones and losing all direction, trapped in that graveyard till the dawn when anyone on the road could see us and the truck too.

But the moon soon enough wipes clear the cloud and we walk on, not more than fifty yards from the caretaker's place when we stop. We're close enough to see the light that's been glowing is his back-porch light. Wesley flares his lighter at the grave to check it's the right one and I see the stone is for both Lieutenant Hutchinson and his wife. His name is on the left so it's easy enough to figure that's the side he's laying on.

"Eighteen and sixty-four," says Wesley, moving the lighter closer to the stone. "I figure a officer killed during the war would for sure be buried in his uniform."

I get the shovel and pickax in my right hand and lean them toward Wesley.

"Your turn," I say.

"I was thinking you could get it started good and then I'd take over," he says.

"I'll do most of it," I say, "but I ain't doing it all."

Wesley sees I aim not to budge and reaches for the pickax. He does it in a careless kind of way and the pickax's spike end clangs against the shovel blade. A dog starts barking down at the caretaker's place and I'm ready to make a run for the truck but Wesley shushes me.

"Give it a minute," he says.

We stand there still as the stones around us. No light inside the shack comes on, and the dog shuts up directly.

"We're okay," Wesley says, and he starts breaking ground with the pickax. He's working in fourth gear and I know he's wanting this done quick as I do.

"I'll loosen the dirt and you shovel it away," Wesley gasps, veins sticking out on his neck like there's a noose around it. "We can get it out faster that way."

Funny you didn't think of that till it was your turn to dig, I'm thinking, but that dog has set loose the fear in me more than any time since we drove up. I take the shovel and we're making the dirt fly, Wesley doing more work in fifteen minutes than he's done in twelve years on the road crew. And me staying right with him, both of us going so hard it's not till we hear a growl that we turn around and see we're not alone.

"What are you boys up to?" the old man asks, waggling his shotgun at us. The dog is haunched up beside him, big and bristly and looking like it's just waiting for the word to pour its teeth into us.

"I said, what are you boys up to?" the old man asks us again.

What kind of answer to give that question is as far beyond me as the moon up above. For a few moments it's beyond Wesley as well but soon enough he opens his mouth, working up some words like you'd work up a good spit of tobacco.

"We didn't know there to be a law against it," Wesley says, which is about the stupidest thing he could have come up with.

The old man chuckles.

"They's several, and you're going to be learning all of them soon as I get the sheriff up here."

I'm thinking to make a run for it before that, take my chances with the dog and the old man's aim if he decides to shoot, because to my way of thinking time in the jailhouse would be worse than anything that dog or old man could do to me.

"You ain't needing to call the sheriff," Wesley says.

Wesley steps out of the two-foot hole we've dug, gets up closer to the old man. The dog growls deep down in its throat, a sound that says don't wander no closer unless you want to limp out of this graveyard. Wesley pays the dog some mind and doesn't go any nearer.

"Why is that?" the old man says. "What you offering to make me think I don't need to call the law?"

"I got a ten-dollar bill in my wallet that has your name on it," Wesley says, and I almost laugh at the sass of him. We have a shotgun leveled at us and Wesley's trying to lowball the fellow.

"You got to do better than that," the old man says.

"Twenty then," Wesley says. "God's truth that's all the money I got on me."

The old man ponders the offer a moment.

"Give me the money," he says.

Wesley gets his billfold out, tilts it so the old man can't see nothing but the twenty he pulls out. He reaches the bill to the old man.

"You can't tell nobody about this," Wesley says. "None but us three knows a thing of it."

"Who am I going to spread it to?" the old man says. "In case you'd not noticed, my neighbors ain't much for conversing."

The old man looks the twenty over careful, like he's figuring it to be counterfeit. Then he folds the bill and puts it in his front pocket.

"Course you could double that easy enough," Wesley says, "not do a thing more than let us dig here a while longer."

The old man takes in Wesley's offer but doesn't commit either way.

"What are you all grubbing for anyways," he says, "buried treasure?"

"Just Civil War things, buckles and such," Wesley says. "No money in it, just kind of a sentimental thing. My great-great-granddaddy fought Confederate. I've always been one to honor them that come before me."

"By robbing their graves," the old man says. "That's some real honoring you're doing."

"I'm wearing what they can't no longer wear, bringing it out of the ground to the here and now. Look here," Wesley says. He unknots the bedsheet and hands the buckle to the old man. "I'll polish it up real good and wear it proud, wear it not just for my great-great-granddaddy but all them that fought for a noble cause."

I've never even seen a politician lie better, because Wesley lays all of that out there slick, figuring the old man has no knowing of the buckle's worth. And that seemed a likely enough thing since I hadn't the least notion myself till Wesley showed me the prices.

The old man fetches a flashlight from his coveralls. He lays its light out on the stone. "North Carolina Sixty-fourth," he reads off the stone. "My folks sided Union," the old man says, "in this very county. Lots of people

don't bother to know that anymore, but there was as
many in these mountains fought Union as Confederate.
The Sixty-fourth done a lot of meanness in this county
back then. They'd shoot a unarmed man and wasn't
above whipping women. My grandma told me all about
it. One of them women they whipped was her own
momma. I read up on it some later. That's how come
me to know it was the Sixty-fourth."

The old man clicks off his flashlight and stuffs it in
his pocket and pulls out an old-timey watch, the kind
with a chain on it. He pops it open and reads the hands
by moonlight.

"Two-thirty," he says. "You fellows go ahead and dig
him up. The way I figure it, his soul's a lot deeper, all the
way down in hell."

"Give him his twenty dollars," Wesley says to me.

I only have sixteen and am about to say so when the
old man tells me he don't want my money.

"I'll take enough pleasure just in watching you dig
this Hutchinson fellow up. He might have been the one
what stropped my great-grandma."

The old man steps back a few feet and perches his
backside on a flat-topped stone next to where we're digging. The shotgun's settled in the crook of his arm.

"You ain't needing for that shotgun to be nosed in
our direction," Wesley says. "Them things can go off by
accident sometimes."

The old man keeps the gun barrel where it is.

"I don't think I've heard the truth walk your lips yet," he tells Wesley. "I'll trust you better with it pointed your way."

We start digging again, getting more crowded up to each other as the hole deepens, but leastways we don't have to worry about noise anymore. We're a good four foot in when Wesley stops and leans his back against the side of the hole.

"Can't do no more," he says, and it takes him three breaths to get just the four words out. "Done something to my arm."

Sure you did, I'm thinking, but when I look at him I can see he's hurting. He's heaving hard and shedding sweat like it's a July noon.

The old man gets off his perch to check out Wesley as well.

"You look to have had the starch took out of you," the old man says, but Wesley makes no bother to answer him, just closes his eyes and leans harder against the grave's side.

"You want to get out," I say to him. "It might help to breathe some fresher air."

"No," he says, opening his eyes some, and I know the why of that answer. He's not getting out until he's looked inside the coffin we're rooting up.

Maybe it's because Lieutenant Hutchinson was buried in May instead of January, but for whatever reason he looks to have got the full six feet. The hole's up to my neck and I still haven't touched wood.

The old man's still there above me, craning his own wrinkly face over the hole like he's peering down a well.

"You ain't much of a talker, are you?" he says to me. "Or is it just your buddy don't give you a word edgewise."

"No," I say, throwing a shovelful of dirt out of the hole.

It's getting harder now after five hours of digging and shucking it out. My back's hurting and my arms feel made of syrup.

"Which *no* you siding with?" the old man says.

"'No, I don't talk much."

"You wanting one of them buckles to wear or you just along for the pleasure of flinging dirt all night?"

"Just here to dig," I answer, glad when he don't say nothing more. I got little enough get-go left to spend it gabbing.

I lift the pickax again and I hit something so solid it almost jars the handle from my hands. That jarring goes up my arms and back down my spine bones like I touched an electric fence. I'm figuring it to be a big rock I'll have to dig out before I can get to the coffin. The thought of tussling with a rock makes me so tired I just want to lay down and quit.

"What is it?" the old man says, and Wesley opens his eyes, watches me take the shovel and scrape dirt to get a better look.

But it's no rock. It's a coffin, a coffin made of cast iron. Wesley crunches up nearer the wall so I can get more dirt out, and what I'm thinking is whoever had to tote that coffin had a time of it, because Momma's cast-iron cooking stove wouldn't lift lighter, and it took four grown men to move that stove from one side of the kitchen to the other.

"I'd always heard they was a few of them planted in this cemetery," the old man says, "but I never figured to see one."

The coffin spries Wesley up some. I dig enough room to the side to set my feet so they're not on the lid. Rust has sealed it, so I take the flat end of the pickax and crack the lid open like you'd crowbar a stuck window. I about break my pickax handle but it finally gives. I get down low but I can't lift the lid off by myself.

"You got to help me," I tell Wesley and he gets down beside me.

It's no easy thing to do and we both have to step lively in hardly no room to keep the lid from sliding off and landing on our feet. Soon as we get it off, Wesley puts his left hand on his right shoulder, and I'm thinking it's some kind of salute or something, but then he starts rubbing his arm and shoulder like it's gone numb on him.

"The Lord Almighty," the old man says, and Wesley and me step some to the side to get where we can see good too.

Unlike the other one, you can tell this was a man. The bones are most together and there's even a hank of red hair on his skull. You can tell he's in a uniform too, raggedy but what's left of the pants and coat is butternut. I look over at Wesley and he's seeing nothing but what's made of metal.

There's plenty to fill up his eyeballs that way. A belt buckle is there with no more than a skiffing of rust on it. Buttons too, looking to be a half dozen. But that's not the best thing. What's best is laying there next to the skeleton, a big old sword and scabbard. Wesley reaches for it. The sword's rusted in but after a couple of tugs it starts to give. Wesley finally grunts it out. He holds the sword out before him and I can see he's figuring what it'll fetch and the grin on his face and the way his eyes light up argue a high price indeed. Then all of a sudden he's seeing something else, and whatever it is he sees isn't giving him the notion to smile anymore. He lets the sword slide out his hand and leans back against the wall, his feet still in the coffin. He slides down then, his back against the wall but his bottom half in the coffin, just sitting there like a man in a jon boat. His eyes are still open but there's no more light in them than the bottom of a coal shaft.

"See if they's a pulse on him," the old man says.

I step closer to Wesley, footlogging the coffin so I won't step on the skeleton. I lay hold of Wesley's wrist but there's no more alive there than in his eyes.

I just stand there a minute. All the bad fixes I've been in are like being in high cotton compared to where I am now. I can't even begin to figure what to do. I'm about to tell the old man to level that shotgun on me and pull the trigger for my brain's not bringing up a better solution.

"I don't reckon he'll be strutting around and playing Johnny Reb with his sword and belt buckle," the old man says. He looks at me and it's easy enough for him to guess what I'm feeling. "You shouldn't get the fantods over this," he says. "His dying on you could be all for the better."

"How do you reckon that?" I ask, because I sure can't figure it that way.

"What if he was speaking the truth when he said we're the only three that knows about this?" the old man says.

"I never said a word."

"I got no doubting about that," the old man says. "Far as I can tell you don't say nothing unless it's yanked out of you like a tooth."

"I don't think he'd have spoke about this," I say. "There's not many that would think good of him if he did, and some might even tell the law. I don't figure him to risk that."

"Then I'd say he's helped dig his own grave," the old man says. "Stout as he is, I don't notion you could get him out of there alone and I'm way too old to help you."

"We might could use a rope," I say. "Pull him out that way."

"And what if you did," the old man says. "You think you can drag that hunk of lard behind you like a little red wagon. Even if you can, where you headed with him?"

That's a pretty good question, because here to the truck is a good half mile. I'd have a better chance of toting a tombstone that far.

"It doesn't seem the right sort of thing to do," I say. "I mean for his kin and such not to never know where he's buried."

"Those that wears the badges ain't always the brightest bulbs," the old man says, "but they won't need the brains of a stump to figure what he and you was up to if they find him here." The old man pauses. "Is that truck his or yours?"

"His."

"You leave that truck by the river and the worst gossip on your buddy there is he was fool enough to get drunk and fall in. You bring the law here they'll know him for a grave robber. Which way you notion his kin would rather recollect him?"

The old man's whittling it down to but one path to follow. I try to find a good argument against him, but

I'm too wore down to come up with anything. The old man takes out his watch.

"It's nigh on four o'clock. You get to filling in and you could get that grave leveled by the shank of morning."

"It's two graves to fill," I say. "We dug another one up the hill a ways."

"Well, get as much dirt in them as you can. Even full up they'll be queer looking with all that fresh dirt on them. I'll have to figure some kind of tall tale for folks that might take notice, but I been listening to your buddy all night so I've picked up some good pointers on how to lie."

I look at the sword and think how the blade maybe killed somebody during the Civil War and in its way killed another tonight, at least the wanting of it did.

"He was lying about this stuff not being worth much," I say. "I need the money so I'm going to sell it, but I'll go halves with you."

"You keep it," the old man says. "But I'll take what's in your partner's wallet. He'll need it no more than the lieutenant there needs that sword."

I pull the wallet from Wesley's back pocket, give it to the old man. He pulls out a ten and two twenties.

"I knew that son of a bitch was lying about having no more money," he says, then throws the wallet back in the hole.

I reach the sword and scabbard up to the old man and then the buckle and buttons. I think how easy it would be for him to rooster that trigger and shotgun me. He leans closer to the hole and I see he's still got that shotgun in his hand and I wonder if he's figuring the same thing, because it'd be easy as shooting a rat in a washtub. He gets down on his creaky old knees, and I guess my fearing is clear to him for he lays down the shotgun and gives me a smile.

"I was just allowing I'd give you some help out of there," he says and offers his hand. "Just don't jerk me in there with you."

I take his hand, a strong grip for all his years, and reach my other hand over the lip. It's one good heave and I'm out.

I fetch the shovel and set to the covering up, dead tired but making good time because I'm figuring if it doesn't get done I'll have some serious jailhouse time to wish I had. Plus it's always easier to fling dirt down than up. I get the hole filled and walk up to the other grave, the shovel and pickax in one hand and the sword and bedsheet in the other. The old man and his dog follow me. I get it half full before the pink of morning skims Bluff Mountain.

"I got to go now," I say. "It's getting near dawn."

"Leave the shovel then," the old man says. "I can fill in the rest. Then I'm going to plant chrysanthemums on the graves, let that be the why of the dirt being rooted up."

I have no plans to find out if that's what he does do. My plan is not to be back here again unless someone's hauling me in a box. I walk on down the hill. It's Sunday so I don't see another soul on the road. I park the truck down by the river, no more than a mile from Marshall. I get my handkerchief out and wipe the steering wheel good and the door handle. Then I high-step it, staying in the woods till I'm to the edge of town. I hunker down there till full light, figuring it's all worked good as I could have hoped. They'll soon find the truck, but no one spotted me near it. Wesley and me never were buddies, never went out to bars together or anything, so there's none likely to figure me in his truck last night. I hide the sword and bedsheet under some leaves to get later. When I cross the road in front of Jackson's Café, I figure I'm home free.

But I'm still careful. I don't go inside, just wait by some trees until I see Timmy Shackleford come out. He doesn't live far from me and I step into the parking lot and ask if he'd mind giving me a ride to my trailer.

"You look like the night rode you hard," Timmy says.

I look in the side mirror and I do look rough.

"Got knee-walking drunk," I say. "Last thing I remember I was with a bunch of fellows in a car and said I needed to piss. They set me by the side of the road and took off laughing. Next thing I know, I'm waking up in a ditch."

That's a better lie than I'd have reckoned to spin and I figure I have picked up some pointers from Wesley. Timmy grins but doesn't say anything else. He lets me out at my trailer and goes on his way. I'm starved and have got enough dirt on me to plant a garden, but I just fall in the bed and don't open my eyes till it's full dark outside. When I come awake it's with the deepest kind of fearing, and for a few moments I'm more scared than any time before in my life. Then my mind settles and I see I'm in the trailer, not still in that graveyard.

Come Monday at work I hear how they found Wesley's truck by the river, and most figure him down there fishing or drinking or both and he fell in and drowned. They drag the river for days but of course nothing comes up.

I wait a month before I try to sell the Civil War stuff, driving all the way to Montgomery, Alabama, to a big CSA convention where a whole auditorium is full of buyers and sellers. Some want certificates of authenticity and such, but I finally find a buyer I can do some business with. A lady at the library has pulled up some prices on the Internet and I've got a good figuring of what my stash is worth. The buyer's only offering half what the value is but he's also not asking for certificates or even my name. I tell him I'll take what he's offering but only if it's cash money. He grumbles a bit about that, then finally says, "Stay here," and goes off and comes back with fifty-two hundred-dollar bills, new bills so crisp and smooth they look starched and ironed.

It's more money than the hospital bill and I give what's left to Momma. That makes what I've done feel less worrisome. I think about something else too, how both them graves had big fancy tombstones of cut marble, meaning those dead Confederates hadn't known much wanting of money in their lives. Now that they was dead there was some fairness in letting Momma have something of what they'd left behind.

The only bad thing is I keep having a dream where that old man has shot me and I'm buried in the hole with Wesley. I'm shot bad but still alive and dirt's piled on me and somewhere up above I hear that old man laughing like he was the devil himself. Every time I dream it, I rear up in bed and don't stop gasping for nearly a whole minute. I've dreamed that same exact dream at least once a month for a year now, and I guess it's likely I'll keep doing so for the rest of my life. There's always a price to be paid for anything you get. I wish it weren't so, for it's a fearsome dream, but if it's the worst to come of all that happened I can live with it.

THE ASCENT

Jared had never been this far before, over
Sawmill Ridge and across a creek glazed
with ice, then past the triangular metal sign
that said SMOKY MOUNTAINS NATIONAL PARK. If it had still
been snowing and his tracks were being covered up,
he'd have turned back. People had gotten lost in this
park. Children wandered off from family picnics, hik-
ers strayed off trails. Sometimes it took days to find
them. But today the sun was out, the sky deep and
blue. No more snow would fall, so it would be easy
to retrace his tracks. Jared heard a helicopter hovering
somewhere to the west, which meant they still hadn't

found the airplane. They'd been searching all the way from Bryson City to the Tennessee line, or so he'd heard at school.

The land slanted downward and the sound of the helicopter disappeared. In the steepest places, Jared leaned sideways and held on to trees to keep from slipping. As he made his way into the denser woods, he wasn't thinking of the lost airplane or if he would get the mountain bike he'd asked for as his Christmas present. Not thinking about his parents either, though they were the main reason he was spending his first day of Christmas vacation out here—better to be outside on a cold day than in the house where everything, the rickety chairs and sagging couch, the gaps where the TV and microwave had been, felt sad.

He thought instead of Lyndee Starnes, the girl who sat in front of him in fifth grade homeroom. Jared made believe that she was walking beside him and he was showing her the tracks in the snow, telling her which markings were squirrel and which rabbit and which deer. Imagining a bear track too, and telling Lyndee that he wasn't afraid of bears and Lyndee telling him she was so he'd have to protect her.

Jared stopped walking. He hadn't seen any human tracks, but he looked behind him to be sure no one was around. He took out the pocketknife and raised it, making believe that the pocketknife was a hunting knife and that Lyndee was beside him. If a bear comes, I'll take care of you, he said out loud. Jared imagined Lyndee reaching out and taking his free arm. He kept the knife out as he walked up another ridge, one whose name he didn't know. He imagined Lyndee still grasping his arm, and as they walked up the ridge Lyndee saying how sorry she was that at school she'd told him he and his clothes smelled bad.

At the ridgetop, Jared pretended a bear suddenly raised up, baring its teeth and growling. He slashed at the bear with the knife and the bear ran away. Jared held the knife before him as he descended the ridge. Sometimes they'll come back, he said aloud.

He was halfway down the ridge when the knife blade caught the midday sun and the steel flashed. Another flash came from below, as if it was answering. At first Jared saw only a glimmer of metal in the dull green of rhododendron, but as he came nearer he saw more, a crumpled silver propeller and white tailfin and part of a shattered wing.

For a few moments Jared thought about turning around, but then told himself that an eleven-year-old who'd just fought a bear shouldn't be afraid to get close to a crashed airplane. He made his way down the ridge, snapping rhododendron branches to clear a path. When he finally made it to the plane, he couldn't see much because snow and ice covered the windows. He turned the passenger side's outside handle, but the door didn't budge until Jared wedged in the pocketknife's blade. The door made a sucking sound as it opened.

A woman was in the passenger seat, her body bent forward like a horseshoe. Long brown hair fell over her face. The hair had frozen and looked as if it would snap off like icicles. She wore blue jeans and a yellow sweater. Her left arm was flung out before her and on one finger was a ring. The man across from her leaned toward the pilot window, his head cocked against the glass. Blood stains reddened the window and his face was not covered like the woman's. There was a seat in the back, empty. Jared placed the knife in his pocket and climbed into the backseat and closed the passenger door. Because it's so cold, that's why they don't smell much, he thought.

For a while he sat and listened to how quiet and still the world was. He couldn't hear the helicopter or even the chatter of a gray squirrel or caw of a crow. Here between the ridges not even the sound of the wind. Jared tried not to move or breathe hard to make it even quieter, quiet as the man and woman up front. The plane was snug and cozy. After a while he heard something, just the slightest sound, coming from the man's side. Jared listened harder, then knew what it was. He leaned forward between the front seats. The man's right forearm rested against a knee. Jared pulled back the man's shirt sleeve and saw the watch. He checked the time, almost four o'clock. He'd been sitting in the backseat two hours, though it seemed only a few minutes. The light that would let him follow the tracks back home would be gone soon.

As he got out of the backseat, Jared saw the woman's ring. Even in the cabin's muted light it shone. He took the ring off the woman's finger and placed it in his jean pocket. He closed the passenger door and followed his boot prints back the way he came. Jared tried to step into his earlier tracks, pretending that he needed to confuse a wolf following him..

It took longer than he'd thought, the sun almost down when he crossed the park boundary. As he came down the last ridge, Jared saw that the pickup was parked in the yard, the lights on in the front room. He remembered it was Saturday and his father had gotten his paycheck. When Jared opened the door, the small red glass pipe was on the coffee table, an empty baggie beside it. His father kneeled before the fireplace, meticulously arranging and rearranging kindling around an oak log. A dozen crushed beer cans lay amid the kindling, balanced on the log itself three red-and-white fishing bobbers. His mother sat on the couch, her eyes glazed as she told Jared's father how to arrange the cans. In her lap lay a roll of tinfoil she was cutting into foot-long strips.

"Look what we're making," she said, smiling at Jared. "It's going to be our Christmas tree."

When he didn't speak, his mother's smile quivered.

"Don't you like it, honey?"

His mother got up, strips of tinfoil in her left hand. She kneeled beside the hearth and carefully draped them on the oak log and kindling.

Jared walked into the kitchen and took the milk from the refrigerator. He washed a bowl and spoon left in the sink and poured some cereal. After he ate Jared went into his bedroom and closed the door. He sat on his bed and took the ring from his pocket and set it in his palm. He placed the ring under the lamp's bulb and swayed his hand slowly back and forth so the stone's different colors flashed and merged. He'd give it to Lyndee when they were on the playground, on the first sunny day after Christmas vacation so she could see how pretty the ring's colors were. Once he gave it to her, Lyndee would finally like him, and it would be for real.

Jared didn't hear his father until the door swung open.

"Your mother wants you to help light the tree."

The ring fell onto the wooden floor. Jared picked it up and closed his hand.

"What's that?" his father asked.

"Nothing," Jared said. "Just something I found in the woods."

"Let me see."

Jared opened his hand. His father stepped closer and

took the ring. He pressed the ring with his thumb and finger.

"That's surely a fake diamond, but the ring looks to be real gold."

His father tapped it against the bedpost as if the sound could confirm its authenticity. His father called his mother and she came into the room.

"Look what Jared found," he said, and handed her the ring. "It's gold."

His mother set the ring in her palm, held it out before her so they all three could see it.

"Where'd you find it, honey?"

"In the woods," Jared said.

"I didn't know you could find rings in the woods," his mother said dreamily. "But isn't it wonderful that you can."

"That diamond can't be real, can it?" his father asked.

His mother stepped close to the lamp. She cupped her hand and slowly rocked it back and forth, watching the different colors flash inside the stone.

"It might be," his mother said.

"Can I have it back?" Jared asked.

"Not until we find out if it's real, son," his father said.

His father took the ring from his mother's palm and placed it in his pants pocket. Then he went into the other bedroom and got his coat.

"I'm going down to Bryson City and find out if it's real or not."

"But you're not going to sell it," Jared said.

"I'm just going to have a jeweler look at it," his father said, already putting on his coat. "We need to know what it's worth, don't we? We might have to insure it. You and your momma go ahead and light our Christmas tree. I'll be back in just a few minutes."

"It's not a Christmas tree," Jared said.

"Sure it is, son," his father replied. "It's just one that's chopped up, is all."

He wanted to stay awake until his father returned, so he helped his mother spread the last strips of tinfoil on the wood. His mother struck a match and told him it was time to light the tree. The kindling caught and the foil and cans withered and blackened, the fishing bobbers melting. His mother kept adding kindling to the fire, telling Jared if he watched closely he'd see angel wings folding and unfolding inside the flames. Angels come down the chimney sometimes, just like Santa Claus, she told him. Midnight came and his father still wasn't back. Jared went to his room. I'll lay down just for a few minutes, he told himself, but when he opened his eyes it was light outside.

He smelled the methamphetamine as soon as he opened his bedroom door, thicker than he could ever remember. His parents had not gone to bed. He could tell that as soon as he came into the front room. The fire was still going, kindling piled around the hearth. His mother sat where she'd been last night, wearing the same clothes. She was tearing pages out of a magazine one at a time, using scissors to make ragged stars she stuck on the walls with Scotch tape. His father sat beside her, watching intently.

The glass pipe lay on the coffee table, beside it four baggies, two with powder still in them. There'd never been more than one before.

His father grinned at him.

"I got you some of that cereal you like," he said, and pointed to a box with a green leprechaun on its front.

"Where's the ring?" Jared asked.

"The sheriff took it," his father said. "When I showed it to the jeweler, he said the sheriff had been in there just yesterday. A woman had reported it missing. I knew you'd be disappointed, that's why I bought you that cereal. Got something else for you too."

His father nodded toward the front door where a mountain bike was propped against the wall. Jared walked over to it. He could tell it wasn't new, some of the blue paint chipped away, one of the rubber handle grips missing, but the tires didn't sag and the handlebars were straight.

"It didn't seem right for you to have to wait till Christmas to have it," his father said. "Too bad there's snow on the ground, but it'll soon enough melt and you'll be able to ride it."

Jared's mother looked up.

"Wasn't that nice of your daddy," she said, her eyes bright and gleaming. "Go ahead and eat your cereal, son. A growing boy needs his breakfast."

"What about you and Daddy?" Jared asked.

"We'll eat later."

Jared ate as his parents sat in the front room, passing the pipe back and forth. He looked out the window and saw the sky held nothing but blue, not even a few white clouds. He thought about going back to the plane, but as soon as he laid his bowl in the sink his father announced that the three of them were going to go find a real Christmas tree.

"The best Christmas tree ever," his mother told Jared.

They put on their coats and walked up the ridge, his father carrying a rusty saw. Near the ridgetop, they found Fraser firs and white pines.

"Which one do you like best, son?" his father asked.

Jared looked over the trees, then picked a Fraser fir no taller than himself.

"You don't want a bigger one?" his father asked.

When Jared shook his head no, his father kneeled before the tree. The saw's teeth were dull but his father finally broke the bark and worked the saw through. They dragged the tree down the ridge and propped it in the corner by the fireplace. His parents smoked the pipe again and then his father went out to the shed and got a hammer and nails and two boards. While his father built the makeshift tree stand, Jared's mother cut more stars from the newspaper.

"I think I'll go outside a while," Jared said.

"But you can't," his mother replied. "You've got to help me tape the stars to the tree."

By the time they'd finished, the sun was falling behind Sawmill Ridge. I'll go tomorrow, he told himself.

On Sunday morning the baggies were empty and his parents were sick. His mother sat on the couch wrapped in a quilt, shivering. She hadn't bathed since Friday and her hair was stringy and greasy. His father looked little better, his blue eyes receding deep into his skull, his lips chapped and bleeding.

"Your momma, she's sick," his father said, "and your old daddy ain't doing too well himself."

"The doctor can't help her, can he?" Jared asked.

"No," his father said. "I don't think he can."

Jared watched his mother all morning. She'd never been this bad before. After a while she lit the pipe and sucked deeply for what residue might remain. His father crossed his arms, rubbing his biceps as he looked around the room, as if expecting to see something he'd not seen moments earlier. The fire had gone out, the cold causing his mother to shake more violently.

"You got to go see Brady," she told Jared's father.

"We got no money left," he answered.

Jared watched them, waiting for the sweep of his father's eyes to stop beside the front door where the mountain bike was. But his father's eyes went past it without the slightest pause. The kerosene heater in the kitchen was on, but its heat hardly radiated into the front room.

His mother looked up at Jared.

"Can you fix us a fire, honey?"

He went out to the back porch and gathered an armload of kindling, then placed a thick log on the andirons as well. Beneath it he wedged newspaper left over from the star cutting. He lit the newspaper and watched the fire slowly take hold, then watched the flames a while longer before turning to his parents.

"You can take the bike down to Bryson City and sell it," he said.

"No, son," his mother said. "That's your Christmas present."

"We'll be all right," his father said. "Your momma and me just did too much partying yesterday is all."

But as the morning passed, they got no better. At noon Jared went to his room and got his coat.

"Where you going, honey?" his mother asked as he walked toward the door.

"To get more firewood."

Jared walked into the shed but did not gather wood. Instead, he took a length of dusty rope off the shed's back wall and wrapped it around his waist and then knotted it. He left the shed and followed his own tracks west into the park. The snow had become harder, and it crunched beneath his boots. The sky was gray, darker clouds farther west. More snow would soon come, maybe by afternoon. Jared made believe he was on a rescue mission. He was in Alaska, the rope tied around him dragging a sled filled with food and medicine. The footprints weren't his but those of the people he'd been sent to find.

When he got to the airplane, Jared pretended to unpack the supplies and give the man and woman something to eat and drink. He told them they were too hurt to walk back with him and he'd have to go and get more help. Jared took the watch off the man's wrist. He set it in his palm, face upward. I've got to take your compass, he told the man. A blizzard's coming, and I may need it.

Jared slipped the watch into his pocket. He got out of the plane and walked back up the ridge. The clouds were hard and granite-looking now, and the first flurries were falling. Jared pulled out the watch every few minutes, pointed the hour hand east as he followed his tracks back to the house.

The truck was still out front, and through the window Jared saw the mountain bike. He could see his parents as well, huddled together on the couch. For a few moments Jared simply stared through the window at them.

When he went inside, the fire was out and the room was cold enough to see his breath. His mother looked up anxiously from the couch.

"You shouldn't go off that long without telling us where you're going, honey."

Jared lifted the watch from his pocket.

"Here," he said, and gave it to his father.

His father studied it a few moments, then broke into a wide grin.

"This watch is a Rolex," his father said.

"Thank you, Jared," his mother said, looking as if she might cry. "You're the best son anybody could have, ain't he, Daddy?"

"The very best," his father said.

"How much can we get for it?" his mother asked

"I bet a couple of hundred at least," his father answered.

His father clamped the watch onto his wrist and got up. Jared's mother rose as well.

"I'm going with you. I need something quick as I can get it." She turned to Jared. "You stay here, honey. We'll be back in just a little while. We'll bring you back a hamburger and a Co-Cola, some more of that cereal too."

Jared watched as they drove down the road. When the truck had vanished, he sat down on the couch and rested a few minutes. He hadn't taken his coat off. He checked to make sure the fire was out and then went to his room and emptied his backpack of school books. He went out to the shed and picked up a wrench and a hammer and placed them in the backpack. The flurries were thicker now, already beginning to fill in his tracks. He crossed over Sawmill Ridge, the tools clanking in his backpack. More weight to carry, he thought, but at least he wouldn't have to carry them back.

When he got to the plane, he didn't open the door, not at first. Instead, he took the tools from the back-pack and laid them before him. He studied the plane's crushed nose and propeller, the broken right wing. The wrench was best to tighten the propeller, he decided. He'd straighten out the wing with the hammer.

As he switched tools and moved around the plane, the snow fell harder. Jared looked behind him and on up the ridge and saw his footprints were growing fainter. He chipped the snow and ice off the windshields with the hammer's claw. Finished, he said, and dropped the hammer on the ground. He opened the passenger door and got in.

"I fixed it so it'll fly now," he told the man.

He sat in the backseat and waited. The work and walk had warmed him but he quickly grew cold. He watched the snow cover the plane's front window with a darkening whiteness. After a while he began to shiver but after a longer while he was no longer cold. Jared looked out the side window and saw the whiteness was not only in front of him but below. He knew then that they had taken off and risen so high that they were enveloped inside a cloud, but still he looked down, waiting for the clouds to clear so he might look for the pickup as it followed the winding road toward Bryson City.

THE WOMAN
WHO BELIEVED
IN JAGUARS

On the drive home from her mother's funeral, Ruth Lealand thinks of jaguars. She saw one once in the Atlanta Zoo and admired the creature's movements—like muscled water—as it paced back and forth, turning inches from the iron bars but never acknowledging the cage's existence. She had not remembered then what she remembers now, a memory like something buried in river silt that finally works free and rises to the surface, a memory from the third grade. Mrs. Carter tells them to get out their *History of South Carolina* textbooks. Paper and books shuffle and shift. Some of the boys snicker, for on the book's first page is a drawing of an Indian woman suckling her child. Ruth opens the book and sees a black-and-white sketch of a jaguar, but for only a moment, because this is not a page they will study today or any other day this school year. She turns to the correct page and forgets what she's seen for fifty years.

But now as she drives west toward Columbia, Ruth again sees the jaguar and the palmetto trees it walks through. She wonders why in the intervening decades she has never read or heard anyone else mention that jaguars once roamed South Carolina. Windows up, radio off, Ruth travels in silence. The last few days were made more wearying because she's had to converse with so many people. She is an only child, her early life long silences filled with books and games that needed no other players. That had been the hardest adjustment in her marriage—the constant presence of Richard, though she'd come to love the cluttered intimacy of their shared life, the reassurance and promise of "I'm here" and "I'll be back." Now a whole day can pass without her speaking a word to another person.

In her apartment for the first time in three days, Ruth drops her mail on the bed, then hangs up the black dress, nudges the shoes back into the closet's far corner. She glances through the bills and advertisements, but stops, as she always does, when she sees the flyer of a missing child. She studies the boy's face, ignoring the gapped smile. If she were to see him, he would not be smiling. Her lips move slightly as she reads of a child four feet tall and eighty pounds, a boy with blond hair and blue eyes last seen in Charlotte. Not so far away, she thinks, and places it in a pocketbook already holding a dozen similar flyers.

No pastel sympathy cards brighten her mail. A personal matter, Ruth had told her supervisor, and out of deference or indifference the supervisor hadn't asked her to explain further. Though Ruth's worked in the office sixteen years, her coworkers know nothing about her. They do not know she was once married, once had a child. At Christmas the people she works with draw names, and every year she receives a sampler of cheeses and meats. She imagines the giver buying one for her and one for some maiden aunt. There are days at the office when Ruth feels invisible. Coworkers look right through her as they pass her desk. She believes that if she actually did disappear and the police needed an artist's sketch, none of them could provide a distinguishing detail.

Ruth walks into the living room, kneels in front of the set of encyclopedias on the bottom bookshelf. When she was pregnant, her mother insisted on making a trip to Columbia to bring a shiny new stroller, huge discount bags of diapers, and the encyclopedias bought years ago for Ruth.

They're for your child now, her mother had said. That's why I saved them.

But Ruth's child lived only four hours. She was still hazy from the anesthesia when Richard had sat on the hospital bed, his face pale and haggard, and told her they had lost the baby. In her drugged mind she envisioned a child in the new stroller, wheeled into some rarely used hospital hallway and then forgotten.

Tell them they have to find him, she'd said, and tried to get up, propping herself on her elbows for a moment before they gave way and darkness closed around her.

Richard had wanted to try again. We've got to move on with our lives, he'd said. But she'd taken the stroller and bags of diapers to Goodwill. In the end only Richard moved on, taking a job in Atlanta. Soon they were seeing each other on fewer and fewer weekends, solitude returning to her life like a geographical place, a landscape neither hostile nor welcoming, just familiar.

That their marriage had come apart was not unusual. All the books and advice columnists said so. Their marriage had become a tangled exchange of sorrow. Ruth knew now that it had been she, not Richard, who too easily had acquiesced to the idea that it always would be so, that solitude was better because it allowed no mirror for one's grief. They could have had another child, could have tried to heal themselves. She'd been the unwilling one.

Ruth rubs her index finger over the encyclopedia spines, reading the time-darkened letters like braille. She pulls the J volume out, a cracking sound as she opens it. She finds the entry, a black-and-white photograph of a big cat resting in a tree: *Range: South and Central America. Once found in Texas, New Mexico, Arizona, but now only rare sightings near the U.S.-Mexico border.*

There is no mention of South Carolina, not even Florida. Ruth wonders for the first time if perhaps she only imagined seeing the jaguar in the schoolbook. Perhaps it was a mountain lion or bobcat. She shelves the encyclopedia and turns on her computer, types *jaguar South Carolina extinct* into the search engine. After an hour, Ruth has found three references to *Southeast United States* and several more to *Florida* and *Louisiana*, but no reference to South Carolina. She walks into the kitchen and opens the phone book. She calls the state zoo's main number and asks to speak to the director.

"He's not here today," the switchboard operator answers, "but I can connect you to his assistant, Dr. Timrod."

The phone rings twice and a man's voice answers.

Ruth is unsure how to say what she wants, unsure of what it is that she wants, other than some kind of confirmation. She tells her name and that she's interested in jaguars.

"We have no jaguar," Dr. Timrod says brusquely. "The closest would be in Atlanta."

Ruth asks if they were ever in South Carolina.

"In a zoo?"

"No, in the wild."

"I've never heard that," Dr. Timrod says. "I associate jaguars with a more tropical environment, but I'm no expert on big cats." His voice is reflective now, more curious than impatient. "My field is ornithology. Most people think parakeets are tropical too, but once they were in South Carolina."

"So it's possible," Ruth says.

"Yes, I guess it's possible. I do know buffalo were here. Elk, pumas, wolves. Why not a jaguar."

"Could you help me find out?"

As Dr. Timrod pauses, she imagines his office—posters of animals on the walls, the floor concrete just like the big cats' cages. Maybe a file cabinet and bookshelves but little else. She suspects the room reeks of pipe smoke.

"Maybe," Dr. Timrod says. "I can ask Leslie Winters. She's our large animal expert, though elephants are her main interest. If she doesn't know, I'll try to do a little research on it myself."

"Can I come by the zoo tomorrow to see what you've found?"

Dr. Timrod laughs. "You're rather persistent."

"Not usually," Ruth says.

"I'll be in my office from ten to eleven. Come then."

Ruth calls her office and tells the secretary she will be out one more day.

The needs of the dead have exhausted her. Too tired to cook or go out, Ruth instead finishes unpacking and takes a long bath. As she lies in the warm, neck-deep water, she closes her eyes and summons the drawing of the jaguar. She tries to remember more. Was the jaguar drawn as if moving or standing still? Were its eyes looking toward her or toward the end of the page? Were there parakeets perched in the palmetto trees above? She cannot recall.

Ruth does not rest well that night. She has trouble falling asleep and when she finally does she dreams of rows of bleached tombstones with no names, no dates etched upon them. In the dream one of these tombstones marks the grave of her son, but she does not know which one.

Driving through rush-hour traffic the next morning, Ruth remembers how she made the nurse bring her son to her when the drugs had worn off enough that she understood what lost really meant. She'd looked into her child's face so she might never forget it, stroking the wisps of hair blond and fine as corn silk. Her son's eyes were closed. After a few seconds the nurse had gently but firmly taken the child from her arms. The nurse had been kind, as had the doctor, but she knows they have forgotten her child by now, that his brief life has merged with hundreds of other children who lived and died under their watch. She knows that only two people remember that child and that now even she has trouble recalling what he looked like and the same must be true for Richard. She knows there is not a single soul on earth who could tell her the color of her son's eyes.

At the zoo the next day, the woman in the admission booth gives Ruth a map, marking Dr. Timrod's office with an X.

"You'll have to go through part of the zoo, so here's a pass," the woman says, "just in case someone asks."

Ruth accepts the pass but opens her pocketbook. "I may stay a while."

"Don't worry about it," the woman says and waves her in.

Ruth follows the map past the black rhino and the elephants, past the lost-and-found booth where the Broad River flows only a few yards from the concrete path. She walks over a wooden bridge and finds the office, a brick building next to the aviary.

Ruth is twenty minutes early so sits down on a nearby bench, light-headed with fatigue though she hasn't walked more than a quarter mile, all of it downhill. On the other side of the walkway a wire-mesh cage looms large as her living room. THE ANDEAN CONDOR IS

THE LARGEST FLYING BIRD IN THE WORLD. LIKE ITS AMERICAN RELATIVES, *VULTUR GRYPHUS* IS VOICELESS, the sign on the cage says.

The condor perches on a blunt-limbed tree, its head and neck thick with wrinkles. When the bird spreads its wings, Ruth wonders how the cage can contain it. She lowers her gaze, watches instead the people who pass in front of her. Her stomach clenches, and she realizes she hasn't eaten since lunchtime yesterday.

She is about to go find a refreshment stand when she sees the child. A woman dressed in jeans and a blue T-shirt drags him along as if a prisoner, their wrists connected by a cord of white plastic. As they pass between her and the condor, Ruth stares intently at the blue eyes and blond hair, the pale unsmiling face. She estimates his height and weight as she fumbles with her pocketbook snap, sifts through the flyers till she finds the one she's searching for. She looks and knows it is him. She snaps the pocketbook shut as the woman and child cross the wooden bridge.

Ruth rises to follow and the world suddenly blurs. The wire mesh of the condor's cage wavers as if about to give way. She grips the bench with her free hand. In a few moments she regains her balance, but the woman and child are out of sight.

Ruth walks rapidly, then is running, the pocketbook slapping against her side, the flyer gripped in her hand like a sprinter's baton. She crosses the wooden bridge and finally spots the woman and child in front of the black rhino's enclosure.

"Call the police," Ruth says to the teenager in the lost-and-found booth. "That child," she says, gasping for breath as she points to the boy, "that child has been kid-napped. Hurry, they're about to leave."

The teenager looks at her incredulously, but he picks up the phone and asks for security. Ruth walks past the woman and child, putting herself between them and the park's exit. She does not know what she will say or do, only that she will not let them pass by her.

But the woman and child do not try to leave, and soon Ruth sees the teenager with two gray-clad security guards, guns holstered on their hips, jogging toward her.

"There," Ruth shouts, pointing as she walks toward the child. As Ruth and the security guards converge, the woman in the blue T-shirt and the child turn to face them.

"What is this?" the woman asks as the child clutches her leg.

"Look," Ruth says, thrusting the flyer into the hands of the older of the two men. The security guard looks at it, then at the child.

"What is this? What are you doing?" the woman asks, her voice frantic now.

The child is whimpering, still holding the woman's leg. The security guard looks up from the flyer.

"I don't see the resemblance," he says, looking at Ruth.

He hands the flyer to his partner.

"This child would be ten years old," the younger man says.

"It's him," Ruth says. "I know it is."

The older security guard looks at Ruth and then at the woman and child. He seems unsure what to do next.

"Ma'am," he finally says to the woman, "if you could show me some ID for you and your child we can clear this up real quick."

"You think this isn't my child?" the woman asks, looking not at the security guards but at Ruth. "Are you insane?"

The woman shakes as she opens her purse, hands the security guard her driver's license, photographs of her family, and two Social Security cards.

"Momma, don't let them take me away," the child says, clutching his mother's knee more tightly.

The mother places her hand on her son's head until the older security guard hands her back the cards and pictures.

"Thank you, ma'am," he says. "I apologize for this."

"You should apologize, all of you," the woman says, lifting the child into her arms.

"I'm so sorry," Ruth says, but the woman has already turned and is walking toward the exit.

The older security guard speaks into a walkie-talkie.

"I was so sure," she says to the younger man.

"Yes, ma'am," the security guard replies, not meeting her eyes.

Ruth debates whether to meet her appointment or go home. She finally starts walking toward Dr. Timrod's office, for no better reason than it is downhill, easier.

When she knocks on the door, the voice she heard on the phone tells her to come in. Dr. Timrod sits at a big wooden desk. Besides a computer and telephone, there's nothing on the desk except some papers and a coffee cup filled with pens and pencils. A bookshelf is behind him, the volumes on it thick, some leather bound. The walls are bare except for a framed painting of long-tailed birds perched on a tree limb, their yellow heads and green bodies brightening the tree like Christmas ornaments, *Carolina Paroquet* emblazoned at the bottom.

Dr. Timrod's youth surprises her. Ruth had expected gray hair, bifocals, and a rumpled suit, not jeans and a flannel shirt, a face unlined as a teenager's. A styrofoam cup fills his right hand.

"Ms. Lealand, I presume."

"Yes," she says, surprised he remembers her name.

He motions for her to sit down.

"Our jaguar hunt cost me a good bit of sleep last night," he says.

"I didn't sleep much myself," Ruth says. "I'm sorry you didn't either."

"Don't be. Among other things I found out jaguars tend to be nocturnal. To study a creature it's best to adapt to its habits."

Dr. Timrod sips from the cup. Ruth smells the coffee and again feels the emptiness in her stomach.

"I talked to Leslie Winters yesterday before I left. She'd never heard of jaguars being in South Carolina, but she reminded me that her main focus is elephants, not cats. I called a friend who's doing fieldwork on jaguars in Arizona. He told me there's as much chance of a jaguar having been in South Carolina as a polar bear."

"So they were never here," Ruth says, and she wonders if there is anything left inside her mind she can believe.

"I'd say that's still debatable. When I got home last night, I did some searching on the computer. A number of sources said their range once included the Southeast. Several mentioned Florida and Louisiana, a few Mississippi and Alabama."

Dr. Timrod pauses and lifts a piece of paper off his desk.

"Then I found this."

He stands up and hands the paper to Ruth. The words *Florida, Georgia, and South Carolina* are underlined.

"What's strange is the source is a book published in the early sixties," Dr. Timrod says. "Not a more contemporary source."

"So people just forgot they were here," Ruth says.

"Well, it's not like I did an exhaustive search," Dr. Timrod says. "And the book that page came from could be wrong. Like I said, it's not an updated source."

"I believe they were here," Ruth says.

Dr. Timrod smiles and sips from the styrofoam cup.

"Now you have some support for your belief."

Ruth folds the paper and places it in her purse.

"I wonder when they disappeared from South Carolina?"

"I have no idea," Dr. Timrod says.

"What about them?" Ruth asks, pointing at the parakeets.

"Later than you'd think. There were still huge flocks in the mid-1800s. Audubon said that when they foraged the fields looked like brilliantly colored carpets."

"What happened?"

"Farmers didn't want to share the crops and fruit trees. A farmer with a gun could kill a whole flock in one afternoon."

"How was that possible?" Ruth asks.

"That's the amazing thing. They wouldn't abandon one another."

Dr. Timrod turns to his bookshelf, takes off a volume, and sits back down. He thumbs through the pages until he finds what he's looking for.

"This was written in the 1800s by a man named Alexander Wilson," Dr. Timrod says, and begins to read. "'Having shot down a number, some of which were only wounded, the whole flock swept repeatedly around their prostrate companions, and again settled on a low tree, within twenty yards of the spot where I stood. At each successive discharge, though showers of them fell, yet the affection of the survivors seemed rather to increase; for after a few circuits around the place, they again alighted near me.'"

Dr. Timrod looks up from the book.

"'The affection of the survivors seemed rather to increase,'" he says softly. "That's a pretty heartbreaking passage."

"Yes," Ruth says. "It is."

Dr. Timrod lays the book on the desk. He looks at his watch.

"I've got a meeting," he says, standing up. He comes around the desk and offers his hand. "Congratulations. You may be on the cutting edge of South Carolina jaguar studies."

Ruth takes his hand, a stronger, more calloused

hand than she'd have expected. Dr. Timrod opens the door.

"After you," he says.

Ruth stands up slowly, both hands gripping the chair's arms. She walks out into the bright May morning.

"Thank you," she says. "Thank you for your help."

"Good luck with your search," Dr. Timrod says.

He turns from her and walks down the pathway. Ruth watches him until he rounds a curve and disappears. She walks the other way. When she comes to where the river is closest to the walkway, Ruth stops and sits on the bench. She looks out at the river, the far bank where the Columbia skyline rises over the trees.

The buildings crumble like sand and blow away. Green-and-yellow birds spangle the sky. Below them wolves and buffalo lean their heads into the river's flow. From the far shore a tree limb rises toward her like an outstretched hand. On it rests a jaguar, blending so well with its habitat that Ruth cannot blink without the jaguar vanishing. Each time it is harder to bring it back, and the moment comes when Ruth knows if she closes her eyes again the jaguar will disappear forever. Her eyes blur but still she holds her gaze. Something comes unanchored inside her. She lies down on the bench, settles her head on her forearm. She closes her eyes and she sleeps.

BURNING BRIGHT

After the third fire in two weeks, the talk on TV and radio was no longer about careless campers. Not *three* fires. Nothing short of a miracle that only a few acres had been burned, the park superintendent said, a miracle less likely to occur again with each additional rainless day.

Marcie listened to the noon weather forecast, then turned off the TV and went out on the porch. She looked at the sky and nothing belied the prediction of more hot dry weather. The worst drought in a decade, the weatherman had said, showing a ten-year chart of August rainfalls. As if Marcie needed a chart when all she had to do was look at her tomatoes shriveled on the vines, the corn shucks gray and papery as a hornet's nest. She stepped off the porch and dragged a length of hose into the garden, its rubber the sole bright green among the rows. Marcie turned on the water and watched it splatter against the dust. Hopeless, but she slowly walked the rows, grasping the hose just below the metal mouth, as if it were a snake that could bite her. When she finished she looked at the sky a last time and went inside. She thought of Carl, wondering if he'd be late again. She thought about the cigarette lighter he carried in his front pocket, a wedding gift she'd bought him in Gatlinburg.

When her first husband, Arthur, had died two falls earlier of a heart attack, the men in the church had come the following week and felled a white oak on the ridge. They'd cut it into firewood and stacked it on her porch. Their doing so had been more an act of homage to Arthur than of concern for her, or so Marcie realized the following September when the men did not come, making it clear that the church and the community it represented believed others needed their help more than a woman whose husband had left behind fifty acres of land, a paid-off house, and money in the bank.

Carl showed up instead. Heard you might need some firewood cut, he told her, but she did not unlatch the screen door when he stepped onto the porch, even after he explained that Preacher Carter had suggested he come. He stepped back to the porch edge, his deep-blue eyes lowered so as not to meet hers. Trying to set her at ease, she was sure, appear less threatening to a woman living alone. It was something a lot of other men wouldn't have done, wouldn't even have thought to do. Marcie asked for a phone number and Carl gave her one. I'll call you tomorrow if I need you, she said, and watched him drive off in his battered black pickup, a chain saw and red five-gallon gas can rattling in the truck bed. She phoned Preacher Carter after Carl left.

"He's new in the area, from down near the coast," the minister told Marcie. "He came by the church one afternoon, claimed he'd do good work for fair wages."

"So you sent him up here not knowing hardly anything about him?" Marcie asked. "With me living alone."

"Ozell Harper wanted some trees cut and I sent him out there," Preacher Carter replied. "He also cut some trees for Andy West. They both said he did a crackerjack job." The minister paused. "I think the fact he came by the church to ask about work speaks in his favor. He's got a good demeanor about him too. Serious and soft-spoken, lets his work do his talking for him."

She called Carl that night and told him he was hired.

Marcie cut off the spigot and looked at the sky one last time. She went inside and made her shopping list. As she drove down the half-mile dirt road, red dust rose in the car's wake. She passed the two other houses on the road, both owned by Floridians who came every year in June and left in September. When they'd moved in, she'd walked down the road with a homemade pie. The newcomers had stood in their doorways. They accepted the welcoming gift with a seeming reluctance, and did not invite her in.

Marcie turned left onto the blacktop, the radio on the local station. She went by several fields of corn and tobacco every bit as singed as her own garden. Before long she passed Johnny Ramsey's farm and saw several of the cows that had been in her pasture until Arthur died. The road forked and as Marcie passed Holcombe Pruitt's place she saw a black snake draped over a barbed-wire fence, put there because the older farmers believed it would bring rain. Her father had called it a silly superstition when she was a child, but during a drought nearly as bad as this one, her father had killed a black snake himself and placed it on a fence, then fallen to his knees in his scorched cornfield, imploring whatever entity would listen to bring rain.

Marcie hadn't been listening to the radio, but now a psychology teacher from the community college was being interviewed on a call-in show. The man said the person setting the fires was, according to the statistics, a male and a loner. Sometimes there's a sexual gratification in the act, he explained, or an inability to communicate with others except in actions, in this case destructive actions, or just a love of watching fire itself, an almost aesthetic response. But arsonists are always obsessive, the teacher concluded, so he won't stop until he's caught or the rain comes.

The thought came to her then, like something held underwater that had finally slipped free and surfaced. The only reason you're thinking it could be him, Marcie told herself, is because people have made you believe you don't deserve him, don't deserve a little happiness. There's no reason to think such a thing. But just as quickly her mind grasped for one.

Marcie thought of the one-night honeymoon in Gatlinburg back in April. She and Carl had stayed in a hotel room so close to a stream that they could hear the water rushing past. The next morning they'd eaten at a pancake house and then walked around the town, looking in the shops, Marcie holding Carl's hand. Foolish, maybe, for a woman of almost sixty, but Carl hadn't seemed to mind. Marcie told him she wanted to buy him something, and when they came to a shop called Country Gents, she led him into its log-cabin interior. You pick, she told Carl, and he gazed into glass cases holding all manner of belt buckles and pocketknives and cuff links, but it was a tray of cigarette lighters where he lingered. He asked the clerk to see several, opening and closing their hinged lids, flicking the thumbwheel to summon the flame, finally settling on one whose metal bore the image of a cloisonné tiger.

At the grocery store, Marcie took out her list and an ink pen, moving down the rows. Monday afternoon was a good time to shop, most of the women she knew coming later in the week. Her shopping cart filled, Marcie came to the front. Only one line was open and it was Barbara Hardison's, a woman Marcie's age and the biggest gossip in Sylva.

"How are your girls?" Barbara asked as she scanned a can of beans and placed it on the conveyor belt. Done slowly, Marcie knew, giving Barbara more time.

"Fine," Marcie said, though she'd spoken to neither in over a month.

"Must be hard to have them living so far away, not hardly see them or your grandkids. I'd not know what to do if I didn't see mine at least once a week."

"We talk every Saturday, so I keep up with them," Marcie lied.

Barbara scanned more cans and bottles, all the while talking about how she believed the person responsible for the fires was one of the Mexicans working at the poultry plant.

"No one who grew up around here would do such a thing," Barbara said.

Marcie nodded, barely listening as Barbara prattled on. Instead, her mind replayed what the psychology teacher had said. She thought about how there were days when Carl spoke no more than a handful of words to her, to anyone, as far as she knew, and how he'd sit alone on the porch until bedtime while she watched TV, and how, though he'd smoked his after-supper cigarette, she'd look out the front window and sometimes see a flicker of light rise out of his cupped hand, held before his face like a guiding candle.

The cart was almost empty when Barbara pressed a bottle of hair dye against the scanner.

"Must be worrisome sometimes to have a husband strong and strapping as Carl," Barbara said, loud enough so the bag boy heard. "My boy Ethan sees him over at Burrell's after work sometimes. Ethan says that girl who works the bar tries to flirt with Carl something awful. Of course Ethan says Carl never flirts back, just sits there by himself and drinks his one beer and leaves soon as his bottle's empty." Barbara finally set the hair dye on the conveyor. "Never pays that girl the least bit of mind," she added, and paused. "At least when Ethan's been in there."

Barbara rang up the total and placed Marcie's check in the register.

"You have a good afternoon," Barbara said.

On the way back home, Marcie remembered how after the wood had been cut and stacked she'd hired Carl to do other jobs—repairing the sagging porch, then building a small garage—things Arthur would have done if still alive. She'd peek out the window and watch him, admiring the way he worked with such a fixed attentiveness. Carl never seemed bored or distracted. He didn't bring a radio to help pass the time and he smoked only after a meal, hand-rolling his cigarette with the same meticulous patience as when he measured a cut or stacked a cord of firewood. She'd envied how comfortable he was in his solitude.

Their courtship had begun with cups of coffee, then offers and acceptances of home-cooked meals. Carl didn't reveal much about himself, but as the days and then weeks passed Marcie learned he'd grown up in Whiteville, in the far east of the state. A carpenter who'd gotten laid off when the housing market went bad, he'd heard there was more work in the mountains so had come west, all he cared to bring with him in the back of his pickup. When Marcie asked if he had children, Carl told her he'd never been married.

"Never found a woman who would have me," he said. "Too quiet, I reckon."

"Not for me," she told him, and smiled. "Too bad I'm nearly old enough to be your mother."

"You're not too old," he replied, in a matter-of-fact way, his blue eyes looking at her as he spoke, not smiling.

She expected him to be a shy awkward lover, but he wasn't. The same attentiveness he showed in his work was in his kisses and touches, in the way he matched the rhythms of his movements to hers. It was as though his long silences made him better able to communicate in other ways. Nothing like Arthur, who'd been brief and concerned mainly with satisfying himself. Carl had lived in a run-down motel outside Sylva that rented by the hour or the week, but they never went there. They always made love in Marcie's bed. Sometimes he'd stay the whole night. At the grocery store and church there were asides and stares. Preacher Carter, who'd sent Carl to her in the first place, spoke to Marcie of "proper appearances." By then her daughters had found out as well. From three states away they spoke to Marcie of being humiliated, insisting they'd be too embarrassed to visit, as if their coming home was a common occurrence. Marcie quit going to church and went into town as little as possible. Carl finished his work on the garage but his reputation as a handyman was such that he had all the work he wanted, including an offer to join a construction crew working out of Sylva. Carl told the crew boss he preferred to work alone.

What people said to Carl about his and Marcie's relationship, she didn't know, but the night she brought it up he told her they should get married. No formal proposal or candlelight dinner at a restaurant, just a flat statement. But good enough for her. When Marcie told her daughters, they were, predictably, outraged. The younger one cried. Why couldn't she act her age, her older daughter asked, her voice scalding as a hot iron.

A justice of the peace married them and then they drove over the mountains to Gatlinburg for the weekend. Carl moved in what little he had and they began a life together. She thought that the more comfortable they became around each other the more they would talk, but that didn't happen. Evenings Carl sat by himself on the porch or found some small chore to do, something best done alone. He didn't like to watch TV or rent movies. At supper he'd always say it was a good meal, and thank her for making it. She might tell him something about her day, and he'd listen politely, make a brief remark to show that though he said little at least he was listening. But at night as she readied herself for bed, he'd always come in. They'd lie down together and he'd turn to kiss her good night, always on the mouth. Three, four nights a week that kiss would linger and then quilts and sheets would be pulled back. Afterward, Marcie would not put her nightgown back on. Instead, she'd press her back into his chest and stomach, bend her knees, and fold herself inside him, his arms holding her close, his body's heat enclosing her.

Once back home, Marcie put up the groceries and placed a chuck roast on the stove to simmer. She did a load of laundry and swept off the front porch, her eyes glancing down the road for Carl's pickup. At six o'clock she turned on the news. Another fire had been set, no more than thirty minutes earlier. Fortunately, a hiker was close by and saw the smoke, even glimpsed a pickup through the trees. No tag number or make. All the hiker knew for sure was that the pickup was black.

Carl did not get home until almost seven. Marcie heard the truck coming up the road and began setting the table. Carl took off his boots on the porch and came inside, his face grimy with sweat, bits of sawdust in his hair and on his clothes. He nodded at her and went into the bathroom. As he showered, Marcie went out to the pickup. In the truck bed was the chain saw, beside it plastic bottles of twenty-weight engine oil and the red five-gallon gasoline can. When she lifted the can, it was empty.

They ate in silence except for Carl's usual compliment on the meal. Marcie watched him, waiting for a sign of something different in his demeanor, some glimpse of anxiety or satisfaction.

"There was another fire today," she finally said.

"I know," Carl answered, not looking up from his plate.

She didn't ask how he knew, when the radio in his truck didn't work. But he could have heard it at Burrell's as well.

"They say whoever set it drove a black pickup."

Carl looked at her then, his blue eyes clear and depthless.

"I know that too," he said.

After supper Carl sat on the porch while Marcie switched on the TV. She kept turning away from the movie she watched to look through the window. Carl sat in the wooden deck chair, only the back of his head and shoulders visible, less so as the minutes passed and his body merged with the gathering dusk. He stared toward the high mountains of the Smokies, and Marcie had no idea what, if anything, he was thinking about. He'd already smoked his cigarette, but she waited to see if he would take the lighter from his pocket, flick it, and stare at the flame a few moments. But he didn't. Not this night. When she cut off the TV and went to the back room, the deck chair scraped as Carl pushed himself out of it. Then the click of metal as he locked the door.

When he settled into bed beside her, Marcie continued to lie with her back to him. He moved closer, placed his hand between her head and pillow, and slowly, gently, turned her head so he could kiss her. As soon as his lips brushed hers, she turned away, moved so his body didn't touch hers. She fell asleep but woke a few hours later. Sometime in the night she had resettled in the bed's center, and Carl's arm now lay around her, his knees tucked behind her knees, his chest pressed against her back.

As she lay awake, Marcie remembered the day her younger daughter left for Cincinnati, joining her sister there. I guess it's just us now, Arthur had said glumly. She'd resented those words, as if Marcie were some grudgingly accepted consolation prize. She'd also resented how the words acknowledged that their daughters had always been closer to Arthur, even as children. In their teens, the girls had unleashed their rancor, the shouting and tears and grievances, on Marcie. The inevitable conflicts between mothers and daughters and Arthur's being the only male in the house—that was surely part of it, but Marcie also believed there'd been some difference in temperament as innate as different blood types.

Arthur had hoped that one day the novelty of city life would pale and the girls would come back to North Carolina. But the girls stayed up north and married and began their own families. Their visits and phone calls became less and less frequent. Arthur was hurt by that, hurt deep, though never saying so. It seemed he aged more quickly, especially after he'd had a stent placed in an artery. After that Arthur did less around the farm, until finally he no longer grew tobacco or cabbage, just raised a few cattle. Then one day he didn't come back for lunch. She found him in the barn, slumped beside a stall, a hay hook in his hand.

The girls came home for the funeral and stayed three days. After they left, there was a month-long flurry of phone calls and visits and casseroles from people in the community and then days when the only vehicle that came was the mail truck. Marcie learned then what true loneliness was. Five miles from town on a dead-end dirt road, with not even the Floridians' houses in sight. She bought extra locks for the doors because at night she sometimes grew afraid, though what she feared was as much inside the house as outside it. Because she knew what was expected of her—to stay in this place, alone, waiting for the years, perhaps decades, to pass until she herself died.

It was mid-morning the following day when Sheriff Beasley came. Marcie met him on the porch. The sheriff had been a close friend of Arthur's, and as he got out of the patrol car he looked not at her but at the sagging barn and empty pasture, seeming to ignore the house's new garage and freshly shingled roof. He didn't take off his hat as he crossed the yard, or when he stepped onto the porch.

"I knew you'd sold some of Arthur's cows, but I

didn't know it was all of them." The sheriff spoke as if it were intended only as an observation.

"Maybe I wouldn't have if there'd been some men to help me with them after Arthur died," Marcie said. "I couldn't do it by myself."

"I guess not," Sheriff Beasley replied, letting a few moments pass before he spoke again, his eyes on her now. "I need to speak to Carl. You know where he's working today?"

"Talk to him about what?" Marcie asked.

"Whoever's setting these fires drives a black pickup."

"There's lots of black pickups in this county."

"Yes there are," Sheriff Beasley said, "and I'm checking out everybody who drives one, checking out where they were yesterday around six o'clock as well. I figure that to narrow it some."

"You don't need to ask Carl," Marcie said. "He was here eating supper."

"At six o'clock?"

"Around six, but he was here by five thirty."

"How are you so sure of that?"

"The five-thirty news had just come on when he pulled up."

The sheriff said nothing.

"You need me to sign something I will," Marcie said.

"No, Marcie. That's not needed. I'm just checking off folks with black pickups. It's a long list."

"I bet you came here first, though, didn't you," Marcie said. "Because Carl's not from around here."

"I came here first, but I had cause," Sheriff Beasley said. "When you and Carl started getting involved, Preacher Carter asked me to check up on him, just to make sure he was on the up and up. I called the sheriff down there. Turns out that when Carl was fifteen he and another boy got arrested for burning some woods behind a ball field. They claimed it an accident, but the judge didn't buy that. They almost got sent to juvenile detention."

"There've been boys do that kind of thing around here."

"Yes, there have," the sheriff said. "And that was the only thing in Carl's file, not even a speeding ticket. Still, his being here last evening when it happened, that's a good thing for him."

Marcie waited for the sheriff to leave, but he lingered. He took out a soiled handkerchief and wiped his brow. Probably wanting a glass of iced tea, she suspected, but she wasn't going to offer him one. The sheriff put up his handkerchief and glanced at the sky.

"You'd think we'd at least get an afternoon thunderstorm."

"I've got things to do," she said, and reached for the screen door handle.

"Marcie," the sheriff said, his voice so soft that she turned. He raised his right hand, palm open as if to offer her something, then let it fall. "You're right. We should have done more for you after Arthur died. I regret that."

Marcie opened the screen door and went inside.

When Carl got home she said nothing about the sheriff's visit, and that night in bed when Carl turned and kissed her, Marcie met his lips and raised her hand to his cheek. She pressed her free hand against the small of his back, guiding his body as it shifted, settled over her. Afterward, she lay awake, feeling Carl's breath on the back of her neck, his arm cinched around her ribs and stomach. She listened for a first far-off rumble, but there was only the dry raspy sound of insects striking the window screen. Marcie had not been to church in months, had not prayed for even longer than that. But she did now. She shut her closed eyes tighter, trying to open a space inside herself that might offer up all of what she feared and hoped for, brought forth with such fervor it could not help but be heard. She prayed for rain.

II

RETURN

(In Memory of Robert Holder)

It had been raining that morning in Charlotte. Only when the bus groaned and sputtered into the high mountains above Lenoir did the first snow-flakes flutter against the windshield, stick a moment before being swept away by the wipers. But here it has snowed for hours, with no sign of letting up. He swings the duffel bag across his back, wincing when the helmet's hard curve bangs his shoulder blade. The bus shudders into first gear and heads on to Boone. Then the only sound is water. He steps onto the bridge and lingers a few moments above the middle fork of the New River. The snow on the banks makes the water look dark and still, like water in a well. A few yards farther downstream Holder Branch, the creek that begins on his family's land, enters the larger stream. His right hand clasps the jacket lapels tight against his neck as he steps off the bridge and begins the two-mile walk up Goshen Mountain.

He wonders how many times he has made this walk in his head the last two years. Six hundred, maybe more? All those nights he'd lain awake in his tent, bare chest covered with sweat as sporadic sniper fire and mortar rounds broke through the whir and drone of insects. Because he knew oceans had currents the same way creeks and rivers did, he'd imagine one drop of water making its way from his home in North Carolina to the green waters of the South Pacific. He would follow that drop of water back to its source—first across the Pacific and on through the Panama Canal, then across the Gulf of Mexico and up the Mississippi to the Ohio River, then the New River, then the New River's middle fork, and finally up Holder Branch. Sometimes he never made it all the way back. Somewhere between what his grandfather called the Boone toll road and his family's farmhouse he would fall asleep.

Snowflakes cling to his lashes. He shakes them free and clasps the jacket collar tighter. It's getting dark and he looks down at his wrist, forgetting his watch is gone, lost or stolen somewhere between the Philippines and North Carolina. He passes the meadow where he and his uncle Abe used to rabbit hunt, then passes his uncle's farmhouse, the tractor that hasn't been driven since June rusting in the barn. No light comes from the windows, his aunt down in Boone with her daughter until warmer weather. The creek is beside the road now, but an icy caul muffles its sound, just as the snow muffles his footsteps. The world is as quiet as the moments after the Japanese sniper fired at him from a palm tree.

He hadn't heard the shot but felt it—a sensation like a metal fist hitting the side of his helmet. Knocked to the ground, he looked up and saw the Japanese soldier eject the spent shell. Though dazed, he managed to raise his own rifle, the BAR wavering in his hand as he emptied his clip. The sniper fell through the fronds, landing on his back, blood pooling on the front of his shirt. The Japanese soldier didn't try to rise, but his right hand slowly reached up and freed a thin silver necklace from under his shirt. He touched something affixed to the chain, touched it as though only to make sure it was still there, then let his hand fall back on the ground. Peterson, the medic, had claimed the Japanese only worshipped their emperor. He'd believed Peterson, because Peterson had a college education and was going to be a doctor once the war was over. But now he saw Peterson was wrong, because around the wounded man's neck was a silver cross.

The dying man spoke. The words didn't sound angry or defiant. By this time the rest of the squad was beside them. Peterson kneeled and jerked open the soldier's shirt and peered in.

"What did he say?" he asked Peterson.

"Hell if I know," Peterson replied. "Probably wants water."

He was offering his canteen to Peterson when the Japanese soldier gave a last exhalation. Peterson jerked the cross and necklace from the dead man's neck.

"Your kill, hillbilly," Peterson said, and offered the cross and necklace. "It's silver. You'll get a couple of dollars for it."

When he hesitated, Peterson smiled.

"If you don't want it, I'll take it."

He took it then.

"I didn't check his pockets," Peterson said as he got up. "You can do that yourself."

Peterson and the rest of the squad walked to where a canopy of palm trees offered more shade. Once alone, he knelt beside the Japanese soldier, his back to the other men.

"Find anything else?" Peterson asked when he'd rejoined the others.

"No," he'd said.

The snow falls harder, drifts forming where the road curves. The snow makes it hard to see and he follows the road as much by memory as sight. The road curves left and the incline steepens. He's breathing hard now, unused to the thin mountain air that grows thinner each step farther up Goshen Mountain. In the Philippines the air had been so humid that it was like breathing water. The day's fading light tinges the snow blue.

The road levels and he can just make out the black spire through the snow and trees, then the wooden building itself. He steps into the churchyard and walks around to the back. He leans on the barbed-wire fence post and looks into the graveyard. He squints and sees the new stone and for a moment cannot shake the uneasy feeling that it is his own, that he's really still in the Philippines, dreaming this, maybe even dying or dead. But it's his uncle's name on the stone, not his.

He steps back onto the road and passes Lawson Triplett's place and then crosses a plank bridge, the creek passing beneath to flow on the road's left side. A ghost can't cross fast-moving water, his father had once told him.

He knows there are mountains in Japan, some so high snow never melts on their peaks. The man he killed could have been from those mountains, a farmer like himself, just as unused to the loud humid island nights as he'd been—a man used to nights when all you heard was the wind. He remembers kneeling beside the Japanese soldier, the cross and necklace clutched in his hand as he'd said a quick prayer. Then he'd wedged his fingers between the dead man's teeth, pried them open enough to slip the cross and necklace onto the rigid tongue.

He trudges past Tom Watson's pasture, a little farther the big beech tree he climbed as a kid. The snow is easing some, and he can see better. The creek runs close to the road, little more than a trickle as it nears its source.

The road curves a last time. On the right side is the barbed wire fence that marks his family's property. He passes above the bottomland where he and his father will plant corn and cabbage in a few months. He imagines the rich black dirt buried deep and silent under the snow, how it's there waiting to nurture the seeds they'll plant.

As he approaches the farmhouse, he sees a candle in the front window, and he knows it has been lit every night for a month, placed there for him, to guide him these last few steps. But he does not go inside, not yet. He walks up to the springhouse and takes his helmet from the duffel bag. He fills the helmet with water and drinks.

INTO THE GORGE

His great-aunt had been born on this land, lived on it eight decades, and knew it as well as she knew her husband and children. That was what she'd always claimed, and could tell you to the week when the first dogwood blossom would brighten the ridge, the first blackberry darken and swell enough to harvest. Then her mind had wandered into a place she could not follow, taking with it all the people she knew, their names and connections, whether they still lived or whether they'd died. But her body lingered, shed of an inner being, empty as a cicada husk.

Knowledge of the land was the one memory that refused to dissolve. During her last year, Jesse would step off the school bus and see his great-aunt hoeing a field behind her farmhouse, breaking ground for a crop she never sowed, but the rows were always straight, right-depthed. Her nephew, Jesse's father, worked in an adjoining field. The first few times, he had taken the hoe from her hands and led her back to her house, but she'd soon be back in the field. After a while neighbors and kin just let her hoe. They brought meals and checked on her as often as they could. Jesse always walked rapidly past her field. His great-aunt never looked up, her gaze fixed on the hoe blade and the dark soil it churned, but he had always feared she'd raise her eyes and acknowledge him, though what she might want to convey Jesse could not say.

Then one March day she disappeared. The men in the community searched all afternoon and into evening as the temperature dropped, sleet crackled and hissed like static. The men rippled outward as they lit lanterns and moved into the gorge. Jesse watched from his family's pasture as the held flames grew smaller, soon disappearing and reappearing like foxfire, crossing the creek and then on past the ginseng patch Jesse helped his father harvest, going deeper into land that had been in the family almost two hundred years, toward the original homestead, the place she'd been born.

They found his great-aunt at dawn, her back against a tree as if waiting for the searchers to arrive. But that was not the strangest thing. She'd taken off her shoes, her dress, and her underclothes. Years later Jesse read in a magazine that people dying of hypothermia did such a thing believing heat, not cold, was killing them. Back then, the woods had been communal, *No Trespassing* signs an affront, but after her death neighbors soon found places other than the gorge to hunt and fish, gather blackberries and galax. Her ghost was still down there, many believed, including Jesse's own father, who never returned to harvest the ginseng he'd planted. When the park service made an offer on the homestead, Jesse's father and aunts had sold. That was in 1959, and the government paid sixty dollars an acre. Now, five decades later, Jesse stood on his porch and looked east toward Sampson Ridge, where bulldozers razed woods and pastureland for another gated community. He wondered how much those sixty acres were worth today. Easily a million dollars.

Not that he needed that much money. His house and twenty acres were paid for, as was his truck. The tobacco allotment earned less each year but still enough for a widower with grown children. Enough as long as he didn't have to go to the hospital or his truck throw a rod. He needed some extra money put away for that. Not a million, but some.

So two autumns ago Jesse had gone into the gorge, following the creek to the old homestead, then up the ridge's shadowy north face where his father had seeded and harvested his ginseng patch. The crop was there, evidently untouched for half a century. Some of the plants rose above Jesse's kneecaps, and there was more ginseng than his father could have dreamed of, a hillside spangled with bright yellow leaves, enough roots to bulge Jesse's knapsack. Afterward, he'd carefully replanted the seeds, done it just as his father had done, then walked out of the gorge, past the iron gate that kept vehicles off the logging road. A yellow tin marker nailed to a nearby tree said U.S. Park Service.

Now another autumn had come. A wet autumn, which was good for the plants, as Jesse had verified three days ago when he'd checked them. Once again he gathered the knapsack and trowel from the woodshed. He also took the .32-20 Colt from his bedroom drawer. Late in the year for snakes, but after days of rain the afternoon was warm enough to bring a rattler or copperhead out to sun.

He followed the old logging road, the green backpack slung over his shoulder and the pistol in the outside pouch. Jesse's arthritic knees ached as he made the descent. They would ache more that night, even after rubbing liniment on them. He wondered how many more autumns he'd be able to make this trip. Till I'm seventy, Jesse figured, giving himself two more years. The ground was slippery from all the rain and he walked slowly. A broken ankle or leg would be a serious thing this far from help, but it was more than that. He wanted to enter the gorge respectfully.

When he got in sight of the homestead, the land leveled out, but the ground grew soggier, especially where the creek ran close to the logging road. Jesse saw boot prints from three days earlier. Then he saw another set, coming up the logging road from the other direction. Boot prints as well, but smaller. Jesse looked down the logging road but saw no hiker or fisherman. He kneeled, his joints creaking.

The prints appeared at least a day old, maybe more. They stopped on the road when they met Jesse's, then also veered toward the homestead. Jesse got up and looked around again before walking through the withered broom sedge and joe-pye weed. He passed a cairn of stones that once had been a chimney, a dry well covered with a slab of tin so rusty it served as more warning than safeguard. The boot prints were no longer discernible but he knew where they'd end. Led the son of a bitch right to it, he told himself, and wondered how he could have been stupid enough to walk the road on a rainy morning. But when he got to the ridge, the plants were still there, the soil around them undisturbed. Probably just a hiker, or a bird watcher, Jesse figured, that or some punk kid looking to poach someone's marijuana, not knowing the ginseng was worth even more. Either way, he'd been damn lucky.

Jesse lifted the trowel from the backpack and got on his knees. He smelled the rich dark earth that always reminded him of coffee. The plants had more color than three days ago, the berries a deeper red, the leaves bright as polished gold. It always amazed him that such radiance could grow in soil the sun rarely touched, like finding rubies and sapphires on the gloamy walls of a cave. He worked with care but also haste. The first time he'd returned here two years earlier he'd felt a sudden coolness, a slight lessening of light as if a cloud had passed over the sun. Imagination, he'd told himself then, but it had made him work faster, with no pauses to rest.

Jesse jabbed the trowel into the loamy soil, probing inward with care so as not to cut the root, slowly bringing it to light. The root was a big one, six inches long, tendrils sprouting from the core like clay renderings of human limbs. Jesse scraped away the dirt and placed the root in the backpack, just as carefully buried the seeds to ensure another harvest. As he crawled a few feet left to unearth another plant, he felt the moist dirt seeping its way through the knees of his blue jeans. He liked being this close to the earth, smelling it, feeling it on his hands and under his nails, the same as when he planted tobacco sprigs in the spring. A song he'd heard on the radio drifted into his head, a woman wanting to burn down a whole town. He let the tune play in his head and tried to fill in the refrain as he pressed the trowel into the earth.

"You can lay that trowel down," a voice behind Jesse said. "Then raise your hands."

Jesse turned and saw a man in a gray shirt and green khakis, a gold badge on his chest and U.S. Park Service patch on the shoulder. Short blond hair, dark eyes. A young man, probably not even thirty. A pistol was holstered on his right hip, the safety strap off.

"Don't get up," the younger man said again, louder this time.

Jesse did as he was told. The park ranger came closer, picked up the backpack, and stepped away. Jesse watched as he opened the compartment with the ginseng root, then the smaller pouch. The ranger took out the .32-20 and held it in his palm. The gun had belonged to Jesse's grandfather and father before being passed on to Jesse. The ranger inspected it as he might an arrowhead or spear point he'd found.

"That's just for the snakes," Jesse said.

"Possession of a firearm is illegal in the park," the ranger said. "You've broken two laws, federal laws. You'll be getting some jail time for this."

The younger man looked like he might say more, then seemed to decide against it.

"This ain't right," Jesse said. "My daddy planted the seeds for this patch. That ginseng wouldn't even be here if it wasn't for him. And that gun, if I was poaching I'd have a rifle or shotgun."

What was happening didn't seem quite real. The world, the very ground he stood on, felt like it was evaporating beneath him. Jesse almost expected somebody, though he couldn't say who, to come out of the woods laughing about the joke just played on him. The ranger placed the pistol in the backpack. He unclipped the walkie-talkie from his belt, pressed a button, and spoke.

"He did come back and I've got him."

A staticky voice responded, the words indiscernible to Jesse.

"No, he's too old to be much trouble. We'll be waiting on the logging road."

The ranger pressed a button and placed the walkie-talkie back on his belt. Jesse read the name on the silver name tag. *Barry Wilson.*

"You any kin to the Wilsons over on Balsam Mountain?"

"No," the younger man said. "I grew up in Charlotte."

The walkie-talkie crackled and the ranger picked it up, said okay, and clipped it back on his belt.

"Call Sheriff Arrowood," Jesse said. "He'll tell you

I've never been in any trouble before. Never, not even a speeding ticket."

"Let's go."

"Can't you just forget this," Jesse said. "It ain't like I was growing marijuana. There's plenty that do in this park. I know that for a fact. That's worse than what I done."

The ranger smiled.

"We'll get them eventually, old fellow, but their bulbs burn brighter than yours. They're not big enough fools to leave us footprints to follow."

The ranger slung the backpack over his shoulder.

"You've got no right to talk to me like that," Jesse said.

There was still plenty of distance between them, but the ranger looked like he contemplated another step back.

"If you're going to give me trouble, I'll just go ahead and cuff you now."

Jesse almost told the younger man to come on and try, but he made himself look at the ground, get himself under control before he spoke.

"No, I ain't going to give you any trouble," he finally said, raising his eyes.

The ranger nodded toward the logging road.

"After you, then."

Jesse moved past the ranger, stepping through the broom sedge and past the ruined chimney, the ranger to his right, two steps behind. Jesse veered slightly to his left, moving so he'd pass close to the old well. He paused and glanced back at the ranger.

"That trowel of mine, I ought to get it."

The ranger paused too and was about to reply when Jesse took a quick step and shoved the ranger with two hands toward the well. The ranger didn't fall until one foot went through the rotten tin, then the other. As he did, the backpack dropped from his hand. He didn't go all the way through, just up to his arms, his fingernails scraping the tin for leverage, looking like a man caught in muddy ice. The ranger's hands found purchase, one on a hank of broom sedge, the other on the metal's firmer edging. He began pulling himself out, wincing as the rusty tin tore cloth and skin. He looked at Jesse, who stood above him.

"You've really screwed up now," the ranger gasped.

Jesse bent down and reached not for the younger man's hand but his shoulder. He pushed hard, the ranger's hands clutching only air as he fell through the rotten metal, a thump and simultaneous snap of bone as he hit the well's dry floor. Seconds passed but no other sound rose from the darkness.

The backpack lay at the edge and Jesse snatched it up. He ran, not toward his farmhouse but into the woods. He didn't look back again but bear-crawled through the ginseng patch and up the ridge, his breaths loud pants.

Trees thickened around him, oaks and poplars, some hemlocks. The soil was thin and moist, and he slipped several times. Halfway up the ridge he paused, his heart battering his chest. When it finally calmed, Jesse heard a vehicle coming up the logging road and saw a pale-green forest service jeep. A man and a woman got out.

Jesse went on, passing through another patch of ginseng, probable descendants from his father's original seedlings. The sooner he got to the ridge crest, the sooner he could make his way across it toward the gorge head. His legs were leaden now and he couldn't catch his breath. The extra pounds he'd put on the last few years draped over his belt, gave him more to haul. His mind went dizzy and he slipped and skidded a few yards down-hill. For a while he lay still, his body sprawled on the slanted earth, arms and legs flung outward. Jesse felt the leaves cushioning the back of his head, an acorn nudged against a shoulder blade. Above him, oak branches pierced a darkening sky. He remembered the fairy tale about a giant beanstalk and imagined how convenient it would be to simply climb off into the clouds.

Jesse shifted his body so his face turned downhill, one ear to the ground as if listening for the faintest footfall. It seemed so wrong to be sixty-eight years old and running from someone. Old age was supposed to give a person dignity, respect. He remembered the night the searchers brought his great-aunt out of the gorge. The men stripped off their heavy coats to cover her body and had taken turns carrying her. They had been silent and somber as they came into the yard. Even after the women had taken the corpse into the farmhouse to be washed and dressed, the men had stayed on his great-aunt's porch. Some had smoked hand-rolled cigarettes, others had bulged their jaws with tobacco. Jesse had sat on the lowest porch step and listened, knowing the men quickly forgot he was there. They did not talk of how they'd found his great-aunt or the times she'd wandered from her house to the garden. Instead, the men spoke of a woman who could tell you tomorrow's weather by looking at the evening sky, a godly woman who'd taught Sunday school into her seventies. They told stories about her and every story was spoken in a reverent way, as if now that his great-aunt was dead she'd once more been transformed back to her true self.

Jesse rose slowly. He hadn't twisted an ankle or broken an arm and that seemed his first bit of luck since walking into the gorge. When Jesse reached the crest, his legs were so weak he clutched a maple sapling to ease himself to the ground. He looked down through the cascading trees. An orange and white rescue squad van had now arrived. Workers huddled around the well, and Jesse couldn't see much of what they were doing but before long a stretcher was carried to the van. He was too far away to tell the ranger's condition, even if the man was alive.

At the least a broken arm or leg, Jesse knew, and tried to think of an injury that would make things all right, like a concussion to make the ranger forget what had happened, or the ranger hurting bad enough that shock made him forget. Jesse tried not to think about the snapped bone being in the back or neck.

The van's back doors closed from within, and the vehicle turned onto the logging road. The siren was off but the beacon drenched the woods red. The woman ranger scoured the hillside with binoculars, sweeping without pause over where Jesse sat. Another green forest service truck drove up, two more rangers spilling out. Then Sheriff Arrowood's car, silent as the ambulance.

The sun lay behind Clingman's Dome now, and Jesse knew waiting any longer would only make it harder. He moved in a stupor of exhaustion, feet stumbling over roots and rocks, swaying like a drunk. When he got far enough, he'd be able to come down the ridge, ascend the narrow gorge mouth. But Jesse was so tired he didn't know how he could go any farther without resting. His knees grated bone on bone, popping and crackling each time they bent or twisted. He panted and wheezed and imagined his lungs an accordion that never unfolded enough.

Old and a fool. That's what the ranger had called Jesse. An old man no doubt. His body told him so every morning when he awoke. The liniment he applied to his joints and muscles each morning and night made him think of himself as a creaky rust-corroded machine that must be oiled and warmed up before it could sputter to life. Maybe a fool as well, he acknowledged, for who other than a fool could have gotten into such a fix.

Jesse found a felled oak and sat down, a mistake because he couldn't imagine summoning the energy to rise. He looked through the trees. Sheriff Arrowood's car was gone, but the truck and jeep were still there. He didn't see but one person and knew the others searched the woods for him. A crow cawed once farther up the ridge. Then no other sound, not even the wind. Jesse took the backpack and pitched it into the thick woods below, watched it tumble out of sight. A waste, but he couldn't risk their searching his house. He thought about tossing the pistol as well but the gun had belonged to his father, his father's father before that. Besides, if they found it in his house that was no proof it was the pistol the ranger had seen. They had no proof of anything really. Even his being in the gorge was just the ranger's word against his. If he could get back to the house.

Night fell fast now, darkness webbing the gaps between tree trunks and branches. Below, high-beam flashlights flickered on. Jesse remembered two weeks after his great-aunt's burial. Graham Sutherland had come out of the gorge shaking and chalk-faced, not able to tell what had happened until Jesse's father gave him a draught of whiskey. Graham had been fishing near the old homestead and glimpsed something on the far bank, there for just a moment. Though a sunny spring afternoon, the weather in the gorge had suddenly turned cold and damp. Graham had seen her then, moving through the trees toward him, her arms outstretched. *Beseeching me to come to her*, Graham had told them. *Not speaking, but letting that cold and damp touch my very bones so I'd feel what she felt. She didn't say it out loud, maybe couldn't, but she wanted me to stay down there with her. She didn't want to be alone.*

Jesse walked on, not stopping until he found a place where he could make his descent. A flashlight moved below him, its holder merged with the dark. The light bobbed as if on a river's current, a river running uphill all the way to the iron gate that marked the end of forest service land. Then the light swung around, made its swaying way back down the logging road. Someone shouted and the disparate lights gathered like sparks returning to their source. Headlights and engines came to life, and two sets of red taillights dimmed and soon disappeared.

Jesse made his way down the slope, his body slant-ways, one hand close to the ground in case he slipped.

BURNING BRIGHT

Low branches slapped his face. Once on level land he let minutes pass, listening for footsteps or a cough on the logging road, someone left behind to trick him into coming out. No moon shone but a few stars had settled overhead, enough light for him to make out a human form.

Jesse moved quietly up the logging road. Get back in the house and you'll be all right, he told himself. He came to the iron gate and slipped under. It struck him only then that someone might be waiting at his house. He went to the left and stopped where a barbed-wire fence marked the pasture edge. The house lights were still off, like he'd left them. Jesse's hand touched a strand of sagging barbed wire and he felt a vague reassurance in its being there, its familiarity. He was about to move closer when he heard a truck, soon saw its yellow beams crossing Sampson Ridge. As soon as the pickup pulled into the driveway, the porch light came on. Sheriff Arrowood appeared on the porch, one of Jesse's shirts in his hand. Two men got out of the pickup and opened the tailgate. Bloodhounds leaped and tumbled from the truck bed, whining as the men gathered their leashes. He had to get back into the gorge, and quick, but his legs were suddenly stiff and unyielding as iron stobs. It's just the fear, Jesse told himself. He clasped one of the fence's rusty barbs and squeezed until pain reconnected his mind and body.

Jesse followed the land's downward tilt, crossed back under the gate. The logging road leveled out and Jesse saw the outline of the homestead's ruined chimney. As he came closer, the chimney solidified, grew darker than the dark around it, as if an unlit passageway into some greater darkness.

Jesse took the .32-20 from his pocket and let the pistol's weight settle in his hand. If they caught him with it, that was just more trouble. Throw it so far they won't find it, he told himself, because there's prints on it. He turned toward the woods and heaved the pistol, almost falling with the effort. The gun went only a few feet before thunking solidly against a tree, landing close to the logging road if not on it. There was no time to find the pistol, because the hounds were at the gorge head now, flashlights dipping and rising behind them. He could tell by the hounds' cries that they were already on his trail.

Jesse stepped into the creek, hoping that doing so might cause the dogs to lose his scent. If it worked, he could circle back and find the gun. What sparse light the stars had offered was snuffed out as the creek left the road and entered the woods. Jesse bumped against the banks, stumbled into deeper pockets of water that drenched his pants as well as his boots and socks. He fell and something tore in his shoulder.

But it worked. There was soon a confusion of barks

and howls, the flashlights no longer following him but instead sweeping the woods from one still point.

Jesse stepped out of the creek and sat down. He was shivering, his mind off plumb, every thought tilting toward panic. As he poured water from the boots, Jesse remembered his boot prints led directly from his house to the ginseng patch. They had ways of matching boots and their prints, and not just a certain foot size and make. He'd seen on a TV show how they could even match the worn part of the sole to a print. Jesse stuffed the socks inside the boots and threw them at the dark. Like the pistol they didn't go far before hitting something solid.

It took him a long time to find the old logging road, and even when he was finally on it he was so disoriented that he wasn't sure which direction to go. Jesse walked a while and came to a park campground, which meant he'd guessed wrong. He turned around and walked the other way. It felt like years had passed before he finally made it back to the homestead. A campfire now glowed and sparked between the homestead and the iron gate, the men hunting Jesse huddled around it. The pistol lay somewhere near the men, perhaps found already. Several of the hounds barked, impatient to get back onto the trail, but the searchers had evidently decided to wait till morning to continue. Though Jesse was too far away to hear them, he knew they talked to help pass the time. They probably had food with them, perhaps coffee as well. Jesse realized he was thirsty and thought about going back to the creek for some water, but he was too tired.

Dew wet his bare feet as he passed the far edge of the homestead and then to the woods' edge where the ginseng was. He sat down, and in a few minutes felt the night's chill envelop him. A frost warning, the radio had said. He thought of how his great-aunt had taken off her clothes and how, despite the scientific explanation, it seemed to Jesse a final abdication of everything she had once been.

He looked toward the eastern sky. It seemed he'd been running a week's worth of nights, but he saw the stars hadn't begun to pale. The first pink smudges on the far ridgeline were a while away, perhaps hours. The night would linger long enough for what would or would not come. He waited.

FALLING STAR

She don't understand what it's like for me when she walks out the door on Monday and Wednesday nights. She don't know how I sit in the dark watching the TV but all the while I'm listening for her car. Or understand I'm not ever certain till I hear the Chevy coming up the drive that she's coming home. How each time a little less of her comes back, because after she checks on Janie she spreads the books open on the kitchen table, and she may as well still be at that college for her mind is so far inside what she's studying. I rub the back of her neck. I say maybe we could go to bed a little early tonight. I tell her there's lots better things to do than study some old book. She knows my meaning.

"I've got to finish this chapter," Lynn says, "maybe after that."

But that "maybe" doesn't happen. I go to bed alone. Pouring concrete is a young man's job and I ain't so young anymore. I need what sleep I can get to keep up.

"You're getting long in the tooth, Bobby," a young buck told me one afternoon I huffed and puffed to keep up. "You best get you one of them sit-down jobs, maybe test rocking chairs."

They all got a good laugh out of that. Mr. Winchester, the boss man, laughed right along with them.

"Ole Bobby's still got some life in him yet, ain't you," Mr. Winchester said.

He smiled when he said it, but there was some serious in his words.

"Yes, sir," I said. "I ain't even got my second wind yet."

Mr. Winchester laughed again, but I knew he'd had his eye on me. It won't trouble him much to fire me when I can't pull my weight anymore.

The nights Lynn stays up I don't ever go right off to sleep, though I'm about nine ways whipped from work. I lay there in the dark and think about something she said a while back when she first took the notion to go back to school. You ought to be proud of me for wanting to make something of myself, she'd said. Maybe it ain't the way she means it to sound, but I can't help thinking she was also saying, "Bobby, just because you've never made anything of yourself don't mean I have to do the same."

I think about something else she once told me. It was Christmas our senior year in high school. Lynn's folks and brothers had finally gone to bed and me and her was on the couch. The lights was all off but for the tree lights glowing and flicking like little stars. I'd already unwrapped the box that had me a sweater in it. I took the ring out of my front pocket and gave it to her. I tried to act all casual but I could feel my hand trembling. We'd talked some about getting married but it had always been in the far-away, after I got a good job, after she'd got some more schooling. But I hadn't wanted to wait that long. She'd put the ring on and though it was just a quarter-carat she made no notice of that.

"It's so pretty," Lynn had said.

"So will you?" I'd asked.

"Of course," she'd told me. "It's what I've wanted, more than anything in the world."

So I lay in the bedroom nights remembering things and though I'm not more than ten feet away it's like there's a big glass door between me and the kitchen table, and it's locked on Lynn's side. We just as well might be living in different counties for all the closeness

I feel. A diamond can cut through glass, I've heard, but I ain't so sure anymore.

One night I dream I'm falling. There are tree branches all around me but I can't grab hold of one. I just keep falling and falling for forever. I wake up all sweaty and gasping for breath. My heart pounds like it's some kind of animal trying to tear out my chest. Lynn's got her back to me, sleeping like she ain't got a care in the world. I look at the clock and see I have thirty minutes before the alarm goes off. I'll sleep no more anyway so I pull on my work clothes and stumble into the kitchen to make some coffee.

The books are on the kitchen table, big thick books. I open up the least one, a book called *Astronomy Today*. I read some and it makes no sense. Even the words I know don't seem to lead nowhere. They just as likely could be ants scurrying around the page. But Lynn understands them. She has to since she makes all As on her tests.

I touch the cigarette lighter in my pocket and think a book is so easy a thing to burn. I think how in five minutes they'd be nothing but ashes, ashes nobody could read. I get up before I dwell on such a thing too long. I check on Janie and she's managed to kick the covers off the bed. It's been a month since she started second grade but it seems more like a month since we brought her home from the hospital. Things can change faster than a person can sometimes stand, Daddy used to say, and I'm learning the truth of that. Each morning it's like Janie's sprouted another inch.

"I'm a big girl now," she tells her grandma and that always gets a good laugh. I took her the first day of school this year and it wasn't like first grade when she was tearing up when me and Lynn left her there. Janie was excited this time, wanting to see her friends. I held her hand when we walked into the classroom. There was other parents milling around, the kids searching for the desk that had their name on it. I looked the room over pretty good. A hornet's nest was stuck on a wall and a fish tank bubbled at the back, beside it a big blue globe like I'd had in my second-grade room. WELCOME BACK was written in big green letters on the door.

"You need to leave," Janie said, letting go of my hand.

It wasn't till then I noticed the rest of the parents already had, the kids but for Janie in their desks. That night in bed I'd told Lynn I thought we ought to have another kid.

"We barely can clothe and feed the one we got," she'd said, then turned her back to me and went to sleep.

It's not something I gnaw on a few weeks and then decide to do. I don't give myself time to figure out it's a bad idea. Instead, as soon as Lynn pulls out of the drive I round up Janie's gown and toothbrush.

"You're spending the night with Grandma," I tell her.

"What about school?" Janie says.

"I'll come by and get you come morning. I'll bring you some school clothes."

"Do I have to?" Janie says. "Grandma snores."

"We ain't arguing about this," I tell her. "Get you some shoes on and let's go."

I say it kind of cross, which is a sorry way to act since it ain't Janie that's got me so out of sorts.

When we get to Momma's I apologize for not calling first but she says there's no bother.

"There ain't no trouble between you and Lynn?" she asks.

"No ma'am," I say.

I drive the five miles to the community college. I find Lynn's car and park close by. I reckon the classes have all got started because there's not any students in the parking lot. There ain't a security guard around and it's looking to be an easy thing to get done. I take my barlow knife out of the dash and stick it in my pocket. I keep to the shadows and come close to the nearest building. There's big windows and five different classrooms.

It takes me a minute to find her, right up on the front row, writing down every word the teacher is saying. I'm next to a hedge so it keeps me mostly hid, which is a good thing for the moon and stars are out. The teacher ain't some old guy with glasses and a gray beard, like what I figured him to be. He's got no beard, probably can't even grow one.

He all of a sudden stops his talking and steps out the door and soon enough he's coming out of the building and I'm thinking he must have seen me. I hunker in the bushes and get ready to make a run for the truck. I'm thinking if I have to knock him down to get there I've got no problem with that.

But he don't come near the bushes where I am. He heads straight to a white Toyota parked between Lynn's Chevy and my truck. He roots around the backseat a minute before taking out some books and papers.

He comes back, close enough I can smell whatever it is he splashed on his face that morning. I wonder why he needs to smell so good, who he thinks might like a man who smells like flowers. Back in the classroom he passes the books around. Lynn turns the books' pages slow and careful, like they would break if she wasn't prissy with them.

I figure I best go ahead and do what I come to do. I walk across the asphalt to the Chevy. I kneel beside the back left tire, the barlow knife in my fist. I slash it deep and don't stop cutting till I hear a hiss. I stand up and look around.

Pretty sorry security, I'm thinking. I've done what I come for but I don't close the knife. I kneel beside the white Toyota. I start slashing the tire and for a second it's like I'm slashing that smooth young face of his. Soon enough that tire looks like it's been run through a combine.

I get in my truck and drive toward home. I'm shaking but don't know what I'm afraid of. I turn on the TV when I get back but it's just something to do while I wait for Lynn to call. Only she don't. Thirty minutes after her class let out, I still ain't heard a word. I get a picture in my mind of her out in that parking lot by herself but maybe not as by herself and safe as she thinks what with the security guard snoring away in some office. I'm thinking Lynn might be in trouble, trouble I'd put her in. I get my truck keys and am halfway out the door when headlights freeze me.

Lynn don't wait for me to ask.

"I'm late because some asshole slashed my tire," she says.

"Why didn't you call me?" I say.

"The security guard said he'd put on the spare so I let him. That was easier than you driving five miles."

Lynn steps past and drops her books on the kitchen table.

"Dr. Palmer had a tire slashed too."

"Who changed his tire?" I ask.

Lynn looks at me.

"He did."

"I wouldn't have reckoned him to have the common sense to."

"Well, he did," Lynn says. "Just because somebody's book-smart doesn't mean that person can't do anything else."

"Where's Janie?" Lynn asks when she sees the empty bed.

"She took a notion to spend the night with Momma," I say.

"How's she going to get to school come morning?" she asks.

"I'll get her there," I say.

Lynn sets down her books. They're piled there in front of her like a big plate of food that's making her stronger and stronger.

"I don't reckon they got an idea of who done it?" I ask, trying to sound all casual.

Lynn gives a smile for the first time since she got out of the car.

"They'll soon enough have a real good idea. The dumb son of a bitch didn't even realize they have security cameras. They got it all on tape, even his license. The cops will have that guy in twenty-four hours. At least that's what the security guard said."

It takes me about two heartbeats to take that in. I feel like somebody just sucker-punched me. I open my mouth, but it takes a while to push some words out.

"I need to tell you something," I say, whispery as an old sick man.

Lynn doesn't look up. She's already stuck herself deep in a book.

"I got three chapters to read, Bobby. Can't it wait?"

I look at her. I know I've lost her, known it for a while. Me getting caught for slashing those tires won't make it any worse, except maybe at the custody hearing.

"It can wait," I say.

I go out to the deck and sit down. I smell the honey-suckle down by the creek. It's a pretty kind of smell that any other time might ease my mind. A few bullfrogs grunt but the rest of the night is still as the bottom of a pond. So many stars are out that you can see how some seem strung together into shapes. Lynn knows what those shapes are, knows them by their names.

Make a wish if you see a falling star, Momma would always say, but though I haven't seen one fall I think about what I'd wish, and what comes is a memory of me and Lynn and Janie. Janie was a baby then and we'd gone out to the river for a picnic. It was April and the river was too high and cold to swim but that didn't matter. The sun was out and the dogwoods starting to whiten up their branches and you knew warm weather was coming.

After a while Janie got sleepy and Lynn put her in the stroller. She came back to the picnic table where I was and sat down beside me. She laid her head against my shoulder.

"I hope things are always like this," she said. "If there was a falling star that would be all I'd wish for."

Then she'd kissed me, a kiss that promised more that night after we put Janie to bed.

But there wasn't any falling star that afternoon and there ain't one tonight. I suddenly wish Janie was here, because if she was I'd go inside and lay down beside her.

I'd stay there all night just listening to her breathe.

You best get used to it, a voice in my head says. There's coming lots of nights you'll not have her in the same place as you, maybe not even in the same town. I look up at the sky a last time but nothing falls. I close my eyes and smell the honeysuckle, make believe Janie's asleep a few feet away, that Lynn will put away her books in a minute and we'll go to bed. I'm making up a memory I'll soon enough need.

THE CORPSE BIRD

Perhaps if work had been less stressful, Boyd Candler would not have heard the owl. But he hadn't slept well for a month. Too often he found himself awake at three or four in the morning, his mind troubled by engineering projects weeks behind schedule, possible layoffs at year's end. So now, for the second night in a row, Boyd listened to the bird's low plaintive call. After a few more minutes he left the bed, walked out of the house where his wife and daughter slept to stand in the side yard that bordered the Colemans' property. The cool late-October dew dampened his bare feet. Jim Coleman had unplugged his spotlight, and the other houses on the street were unlit except for a couple of porch lights. The subdivision was quiet and still as Boyd waited like a man in a doctor's office expecting a dreaded diagnosis. In a few minutes it came. The owl called again from the scarlet oak behind the Colemans' house, and Boyd knew with utter certainty that if the bird stayed in the tree another night someone would die.

Boyd Candler had grown up among people who believed the world could reveal all manner of things if you paid attention. As a child he'd watched his grandfather, the man he and his parents lived with, find a new well for a neighbor with nothing more than a branch from an ash tree. He'd been in the neighbor's pasture as his grandfather walked slowly from one fence to the other, the branch's two forks gripped like reins, not stopping until the tip wavered and then dipped toward the ground as if yanked by an invisible hand. He'd watched the old man live his life "by the signs." Whether a moon waxed or waned decided when the crops were planted and harvested, the hogs slaughtered, and the timber cut, even when a hole was best dug. A red sunrise meant coming rain, as did the call of a raincrow. Other signs that were harbingers of a new life, and a life about to end.

Boyd was fourteen when he heard the corpse bird in the woods behind the barn. His grandfather had been sick for months but recently rallied, gaining enough strength to leave his bed and take short walks around the farm. The old man had heard the owl as well, and it was a sound of reckoning to him as final as the thump of dirt clods on his coffin.

It's come to fetch me, the old man had said, and Boyd hadn't the slightest doubt it was true. Three nights the bird called from the woods behind the barn. Boyd had been in his grandfather's room those nights, had been there when his grandfather let go of his life and followed the corpse bird into the darkness.

The next morning at breakfast Boyd didn't mention the owl to his wife or daughter. What had seemed a certainty last night was more tenuous in daylight. His mind drifted toward a project due by the week's end. Boyd finished his second cup of coffee and checked his watch.

"Where's Jennifer?" he asked his wife. "It's our week to carpool."

"No pickup today," Laura said. "Janice called while you were in the shower. Jennifer ran a temperature over a hundred all weekend. It hasn't broken so Janice is staying home with her."

Boyd felt a cold dark wave of disquiet pass through him.

"Have they been to the doctor?"

"Of course," Laura said.

"What did the doctor say was wrong with Jennifer?"

"Just a virus, something going around," Laura said, her back to him as she packed Allison's lunch.

"Did the doctor tell Janice anything else to watch out for?" Boyd asked.

Laura turned to him. The expression on her face wavered between puzzlement and irritation.

"It's a virus, Boyd. That's all it is."

"I'll be outside when you're ready," Boyd told his daughter, and walked out into the yard.

The neighborhood seemed less familiar, as though many months had passed since he'd seen it. The subdivision had been built over a cotton field. A few fledgling dogwoods and maples had been planted in some yards, but the only big tree was the scarlet oak that grew on an undeveloped lot behind the Colemans' house. Boyd assumed it was once a shade tree, a place for cotton field workers to escape the sun a few minutes at lunch and water breaks.

The owl was still in the oak. Boyd knew this because growing up he'd heard the older folks say a corpse bird always had to perch in a big tree. It was one way you could tell it from a regular barn or screech owl. Another way was that the bird returned to the same tree, the same branch, each of the three nights.

His family had moved to Asheville soon after his

grandfather's death. Boyd had been an indifferent student in Madison County, assuming he'd become a
farmer, but the farm had been sold, the money divided
among his father and aunts. At Asheville High Boyd
mastered a new kind of knowledge, one of theorems
and formulas, a knowledge where everything could be
explained down to the last decimal point. His teachers
told him he should be an engineer and helped Boyd get
loans and scholarships so he could be the first in his
family to attend college. His teachers urged him into a
world where the sky did not matter, where land did not
blacken your nails, cling to your boots, or callous your
hands but was seen, if at all, through the glass windows
of buildings and cars and planes. The world irrelevant
and mute. His teachers had believed he could leave the
world he had grown up in, and perhaps he had believed
it as well.

Boyd remembered the morning his college sociol-
ogy class watched a film about the folklore of Hmong
tribesmen in Laos. After the film the professor asked if
similar beliefs could be found in other cultures. Boyd
raised his hand. When he'd finished speaking, the professor and the other students stared at Boyd as if a bone
pierced his nostrils and human teeth dangled from his
neck.

"So you've actually witnessed such things?" the professor asked.

"Yes, sir," he replied, knowing his face had turned a deep crimson.

A student sitting behind him snickered.

"And this folklore, you believe in it?" the professor asked.

"I'm just saying I once knew people who did," Boyd said. "I wasn't talking about myself."

"Superstition is nothing more than ignorance of cause and effect," the student behind him said.

Rational. Educated. Enlightened. Boyd knew the same words he'd heard years ago in college, the same sensibility that came with those words, prevailed in the subdivision. Most of his neighbors were transplants from the Northeast or Midwest, all white-collar professionals like himself. His neighbors would assume that since it was October the owl was migrating. Like the occasional possum or raccoon, the owl would be nothing more to them than a bit of nature that had managed to stray into the city and would soon return to its proper environment.

But Boyd did worry, off and on all morning and afternoon. He couldn't remember Allison ever having a fever that lasted three days. He thought about calling the Colemans' house to check on Jennifer, but Boyd knew how strange that would seem. Despite the carpool and their daughters' friendship, the parents' interactions were mostly hand waves and brief exchanges about pickup times. In their six years as neighbors, the two families had never shared a meal.

Though Boyd had work that he'd normally stay late to finish, at five sharp he logged off his computer and drove home. Halloween was five nights away, and as he turned into the subdivision he saw hollow-eyed pumpkins on porches and steps. A cardboard witch on a broomstick dangled from a tree limb, turning with the wind like a weather vane. At another house a skeleton shuddered above a carport, one bony finger extended as if beckoning. A neighborhood contest of sorts, and one that Jim Coleman particularly enjoyed. Each year Jim glued a white bedsheet over a small parade float. He tethered its nylon cord to a concrete block so that his makeshift ghost hovered over the Coleman house.

There had been no such displays when Boyd was a child, no dressing up to trick-or-treat. Perhaps because the farm was so isolated, but Boyd now suspected it had been more an understanding that certain things shouldn't be mocked, that to do so might bring retribution. As Boyd passed another house, this one adorned with black cats, he wondered if that retribution had already come, was perched in the scarlet oak.

It was almost dark when he pulled into the driveway behind his wife's Camry. Through the front window,

Boyd saw Allison sprawled in front of the fire, Laura sitting on the couch. The first frost of the year had been predicted for tonight and from the chill in the air Boyd knew it would be so.

He stepped into the side yard and studied the Colemans' house. Lights were on in two rooms upstairs as well as in the kitchen and dining room. Both vehicles were in the carport. Jim Coleman had turned on a spotlight he'd set on the roof, and it illuminated the ghost looming overhead.

Boyd walked into the backyard. The scarlet oak's leaves caught the day's last light. *Lambent*, that was the word for it, Boyd thought, like red wine raised to candlelight. He slowly raised his gaze but did not see the bird. He clapped his hands together, so hard his palms burned. Something dark lifted out of the tallest limb, hung above the tree a moment, then resettled.

In the living room, Allison and her schoolbooks lay sprawled in front of the hearth. When Boyd leaned to kiss her he felt the fire's warmth on her face. Laura sat on the couch, writing month-end checks.

"How is Jennifer?" he asked when he came into the kitchen.

Laura set the checkbook aside.

"No better. Janice called and said she was going to keep her home again tomorrow."

"Did she take her back to the doctor?"

"Yes. The doctor gave her some antibiotics and took a strep culture."

Allison twisted her body and turned to Boyd.

"You need to cut us some more wood this weekend, Daddy. There are only a few big logs left."

Boyd nodded and let his eyes settle on the fire. Laura had wanted to switch to gas logs. Just like turning a TV on and off, that easy, his wife had said, and a lot less messy. Boyd had argued the expense, especially since the wood he cut was free, but it was more than that. Cutting the wood, stacking, and finally burning it gave him pleasure, work that, unlike so much of what he did at his job, was tactile, somehow more real.

Boyd was staring at the hearth when he spoke.

"I think Jennifer needs to see somebody else, somebody besides a family doctor."

"Why do you think that, Daddy?" Allison asked.

"Because I think she's real sick."

"But she can't miss Halloween," Allison said. "We're both going to be ghosts."

"How can you know that?" Laura asked. "You haven't even seen her."

"I just know."

Laura was about to say something else, then hesitated.

"We'll talk about this later," Laura said.

H e waited until after supper to knock on the Colemans' door. Laura had told him not to go, but
Boyd went anyway. Jim Coleman opened the door.
Boyd stood before a man he suddenly realized he knew
hardly anything about. He didn't know how many sib-
lings Jim Coleman had or what kind of neighborhood in
Chicago he'd grown up in or if he'd ever held a shotgun
or hoe in his hand. He did not know if Jim Coleman had
once been a churchgoer or had always spent his Sunday
mornings working in his garage or yard.

"I've come to check on Jennifer," Boyd said.

"She's sleeping," Jim answered.

"I'd still like to see her, if you don't mind," Boyd said,
and showed Jim a sheet of paper. "I had Allison write
down what they did in class today. She'd be real disappointed if I didn't deliver this."

For a moment Boyd thought he would say no, but
Jim Coleman stepped aside.

"Come in then."

He followed Jim down the hallway and up the stairs
to Jennifer's bedroom. The girl lay in her bed, the sheets
pulled up to her neck. Sweat had matted the child's hair,
made her face a shiny paleness, like porcelain. In a few
moments Janice joined them. She pressed her palm
against Jennifer's forehead and let it linger as though
bestowing a blessing on the child.

"What was her temperature the last time you checked?" Boyd asked.

"One hundred and two. It goes up in the evening."

"And it's been four days now?"

"Yes," Janice said. "Four days and four nights. I let her go to school Friday. I probably shouldn't have."

Boyd looked at Jennifer. He tried to put himself in her parents' situation. He tried to imagine what words could connect what he'd witnessed in Madison County to some part of their experience in Chicago or Raleigh. But there were no such words. What he had learned in the North Carolina mountains was untranslatable to the Colemans.

"I think you need to get her to the hospital," Boyd said.

"But the doctor says as soon as the antibiotics kick in she'll be fine," Janice said.

"You need to get her to the hospital," Boyd said again.

"How can you know that?" Janice asked. "You're not a doctor."

"When I was a boy, I saw someone sick like this." Boyd hesitated. "That person died."

"Doctor Underwood said she'd be fine," Jim said, "that plenty of kids have had this. He's seen her twice."

"You're scaring me," Janice said.

"I'm not trying to scare you," Boyd said. "Please take Jennifer to the hospital. Will you do that?"

Janice turned to her husband.

"Why is he saying these things?"

"You need to leave," Jim Coleman said.

"Please," Boyd said. "I know what I'm talking about."

"Leave. Leave now," Jim Coleman said.

Boyd walked back into his own yard. For a few minutes he stood there. The owl did not call but he knew it roosted in the scarlet oak, waiting.

"Janice just called and she's royally pissed off," Laura told him when he entered the house. "I told you not to go over there. They think you're mentally disturbed, maybe even dangerous."

Laura sat on the couch, and she motioned for Boyd to sit down also.

"Where's Allison?" Boyd asked.

"I put her to bed," Laura said. "You know, you're upsetting Allison as well as the Colemans. You're upsetting me too. Tell me what this is about, Boyd."

For half an hour he tried to explain. When Boyd finished his wife placed one of her hands over his.

"I know where you grew up that people, uneducated people, believed such things." Laura said when he'd finished. "But you don't live in Madison County anymore, and you are educated. Maybe there is an owl out back.

I haven't heard it, but I'll concede it could be out there. But even so it's an *owl*, nothing more."

Laura squeezed his hand.

"I'm getting you an appointment with Doctor Harmon. He'll prescribe some Ambien so you can get some rest, maybe something else for the anxiety."

Later that night he lay in bed, waiting for the owl to call. An hour passed on the red digits of the alarm clock and he tried to muster hope that the bird had left. He finally fell asleep for a few minutes, long enough to dream about his grandfather. They were in Madison County, in the farmhouse. Boyd was in the front room by himself, waiting though he didn't know what for. Finally, the old man came out of his bedroom, dressed in his brogans and overalls, a sweat rag in his back pocket.

The corpse bird's call roused him from the dream. Boyd put on pants and shoes and a sweatshirt. He took a flashlight from the kitchen drawer and went into the basement to get the chain saw. The machine was almost forty years old, a relic, heavy and cumbersome, its teeth dulled by decades of use. But it still ran well enough to keep them in firewood.

Boyd filled the gas tank and checked the spark plug and chain lube. The chain saw had belonged to his grandfather, had been used by the old man to cull trees from his farm for firewood. Boyd had often gone into the woods with him, helped load the logs and kindling into his grandfather's battered pickup. After the old man's health had not allowed him to use it anymore, he'd given it to Boyd. Two decades had passed before he found a use for it. A coworker owned some thirty acres near Cary and offered Boyd all the free wood he wanted as long as the trees were dead and Boyd cut them himself.

Outside, the air was sharp and clear. The stars seemed more defined, closer. A bright orange harvest moon rose in the west. He clicked on the flashlight and let its beam trace the upper limbs until he saw it. Despite being bathed in light, the corpse bird did not stir. Rigid as a gravestone, Boyd thought. The unblinking yellow eyes stared toward the Colemans' house, and Boyd knew these were the same eyes that had fixed themselves on his grandfather.

Boyd laid the flashlight on the grass, its beam aimed at the scarlet oak's trunk. He pulled the cord and the machine trembled to life. Its vibration shook his whole upper body. Boyd stepped close to the tree, extending his arms, the machine's weight tensing his biceps and forearms.

The scrub trees on his coworker's land had come down quickly and easily. But he'd never cut a tree the size of the scarlet oak. A few bark shards flew out as the blade hit the tree, then the blade skittered down the trunk until Boyd pulled it away and tried again.

It took eight attempts before he made the beginnings of a wedge in the tree. He was breathing hard, the weight of the saw straining his arms, his back, and even his legs as he steadied not only himself but the machine. He angled the blade as best he could to widen the wedge. By the time he finished the first side, sawdust and sweat stung his eyes. His heart banged against his ribs as if caged.

Boyd thought about resting a minute but when he looked back at the Colemans' house, he saw lights on. He carried the saw to the other side of the trunk. Three times the blade hit the bark before finally making a cut. Boyd glanced behind him again and saw Jim Coleman coming across the yard, his mouth open and arms gesturing.

Boyd eased the throttle and let the chain saw idle.

"What in God's name are you doing," Jim shouted.

"What's got to be done," Boyd said.

"I've got a sick daughter and you woke her up."

"I know that," Boyd said.

Jim Coleman reached a hand out as though to wrest the chain saw from Boyd's hand. Boyd shoved the throttle and waved the blade between him and Jim Coleman.

"I'm calling the police," Jim Coleman shouted.

Laura was outside now as well. She and Jim Coleman spoke to each other a few moments before Jim went into his house. When Laura approached Boyd screamed at her to stay away. Boyd made a final thrust deep into the tree's heart. He dropped the saw and stepped back. The oak wavered a moment, then came crashing down. As it fell, something beaked and winged passed near Boyd's face. He picked up the flashlight and shone it on the bird as it crossed over the vacant lot, disappeared into the darkness it had been summoned from. Boyd sat down on the scarlet oak's stump and clicked off the flashlight.

His wife and neighbor stood beside each other in the Colemans' backyard. They spoke softly to each other, as though Boyd were a wild animal they didn't want to reveal their presence to.

Soon blue lights splashed against the sides of the two houses. Other neighbors joined Jim Coleman and Laura in the backyard. The policeman talked to Laura a few moments. She nodded once and turned in Boyd's direction, her face wet with tears. The policeman spoke into a walkie-talkie and then started walking toward him, handcuffs clinking in the policeman's hands. Boyd stood up and held his arms out before him, both palms upturned, like a man who's just set something free.

WAITING FOR THE
END OF THE WORLD

S o it's somewhere between Saturday night
and Sunday morning clockwise, and I'm in
a cinder-block roadhouse called The Last
Chance, and I'm playing "Free Bird" for the fifth time
tonight but I'm not thinking of Ronnie Van Zant but
an artist dredged up from my former life, Willie Yeats,
and his line *surely some revelation is at hand*. But the
only rough beast slouching toward me is my rhythm
guitar player, Sammy Griffen, who is down on all
fours, weaving through the crowd of tables between
the bathroom and stage.

One of the great sins of the sixties was introducing

drugs to the good-ole-boy element of Southern society. If you were some Harvard psychology professor like Timothy Leary, drugs might well expand your consciousness, but they worked just the opposite way for people like Sammy, shriveling the brain to a reptilian level of aggression and paranoia.

There is no telling what Sammy has snorted or swallowed in the bathroom, but his pupils have expanded to the size of dimes. He passes a table and sees a bare leg, a female leg, and grabs hold. He takes off an attached high heel and starts licking the foot. It takes about three seconds for a bigger foot with a steel-capped toe to swing into the back of Sammy's head like a football player kicking an extra point. Sammy curls up in a fetal position and blacks out among the peanut shells and cigarette butts.

So now it's just my bass player Bobo Lingafelt, Hal Deaton, my drummer, and me. I finish "Free Bird" so that means the next songs are my choice. They got to have "Free Bird" at least once an hour, Rodney said when he hired me, saying it like his clientele were diabetics needing insulin. The rest of the time you play what you want, he'd added.

I turn to Bobo and Hal and play the opening chords of Gary Stewart's "Roarin'" and they fall in. Stewart was one of this country's neglected geniuses, once dubbed honky-tonk's "white trash ambassador from hell" by one of the few critics who bothered listening to him. His music is two centuries' worth of pent-up Appalachian soul, too intense and pure for Nashville, though they tried their best to pith his brain with cocaine, put a cowboy hat on his head, and make him into another talentless music-city hack. Stewart spent some of his last years hunkered down in a North Florida trailer park: no phone, not answering the door, every window of the hulk of rusting tin he called home painted black. Surviving on what songwriting residuals dribbled in from Nashville.

Such a lifestyle has its appeals, especially tonight as I look out at the human wreckage filling The Last Chance. One guy has his head on a table, eyes closed, vomit drooling from his mouth. Another pulls out his false teeth and clamps them on the ear of a gal at the next table. An immense woman in a purple jumpsuit is crying while another woman screams at her. And what I'm thinking is maybe it's time to halt all human reproduction. Let God or evolution or whatever put us here in the first place start again from scratch, because this isn't working.

Like Stewart, I too live in a trailer, but I have to leave it more often than I wish because I am not a musical genius, just a forty-year-old ex-high-school English teacher who has to make money, more than I get from a part-time job proofing copy for the weekly newspaper.

Which is why I'm here from seven to two four nights a week, getting it done in the name of Lynyrd Skynyrd, alimony, and keeping the repo man away from my truck.

I will not bore you with the details of lost teaching jobs, lost wife, and lost child. Mistakes were made, as the politicos say. The last principal I worked for made sure I can't get a teaching job anywhere north of the Amazon rain forest. My ex-wife and my kid are in California. All I am to them is an envelope with a check in it.

Beyond the tables of human wreckage I see Hubert McClain sitting at the bar, beer in one hand and Louisville Slugger in the other. Hubert is our bouncer, two hundred and fifty pounds of atavistic Celtic violence coiled and ready to happen. On the front of the ball cap covering his survivalist buzz cut, a leering skeleton waves a sickle in one hand and a black-and-white checkered victory flag in the other. The symbolism is unclear, except that anyone wearing such a cap, especially while gripping a thirty-six-ounce ball bat, is not someone you want to displease.

Sitting beside Hubert is his best friend, Joe Don Byers, formally Yusef Byers before he had his first name legally changed. While it seems every white male between fourteen and twenty-five is trying to look and act black, Joe Don is going the opposite way, a twenty-three-year-old black man trying to be a Skoal-dipping, country-music-listening good ole boy. But like the white kids with their ball caps turned sideways and pants hanging halfway down their asses, Joe Don can't quite pull it off. The hubcap-sized belt buckle and snakeskin boots pass muster, but he wears his Stetson low over his right eye, the brim's rakish tilt making him look more like a cross-dressing pimp than a cowboy. His truck is another giveaway, a Toyota two-wheel drive with four mud grips and a Dale Earnhardt sticker on the back windshield, unaware that any true Earnhardt fan would rather ride a lawn mower than drive anything other than a Chevy.

On the opposite side of the bar, Rodney is taking whatever people hand him—crumpled bills, handfuls of nickels and dimes, payroll checks, wedding rings, wristwatches. One time a guy offered a gold filling he'd dug out of his mouth with a pocketknife. Rodney didn't even blink.

Watching him operate, it's easy to believe Rodney's simply an updated version of Flem Snopes, the kind of guy whose first successful business venture is showing photos of his naked sister to his junior high peers. But that's not the case at all. Rodney graduated from the University of South Carolina with a degree in social work. He wanted to make the world better, but, according to Rodney, the world wasn't interested.

His career as a social worker ended the same week it began. Rodney had borrowed a church bus to take some of Columbia's disadvantaged youth to a Braves game.

Halfway to Atlanta the teenagers mutinied. They beat Rodney with a tire iron, took his money and clothes, and left him naked and bleeding in a ditch. A week later, the same day Rodney got out of the hospital, the bus was found half submerged in the Okefenokee Swamp. It took another month to round up the youths, several of whom had procured entry-level positions in a Miami drug cartel.

Rodney says running The Last Chance is a philosophical statement. Above the cash register he's plastered one of those Darwinian bumper stickers with the fish outline and four evolving legs. Rodney's drawn a speech bubble in front of the fish's mouth. *Exterminate the brutes,* the fish says.

Advice Rodney seems to have taken to heart. There's only one mixed drink in The Last Chance, what Rodney calls the Terminator. It's six ounces of Jack Daniel's and six ounces of Surrey County moonshine and six ounces of Sam's Choice tomato juice. Some customers claim a dash of lighter fluid is added for good measure. No one, not even Hubert, has ever drunk more than three of these and remained standing. It usually takes only two to put the drinkers onto the floor, tomato juice dribbling down their chins like they've been shot in the mouth.

When we finish "Roarin'" only three or four people clap. A lot of the crowd doesn't know the song or, for that matter, who Gary Stewart was. Radio and Music Television have anesthetized them to the degree that they can't recognize the real thing, even when it comes from their own gene pool.

And speaking of gene pools, I suddenly see Everette Evans, the man that, to my immense regret, is twenty-five percent of the genetic makeup of my son. He's standing in the doorway, a camcorder in his hands. Everette lingers on Hubert a few seconds, then the various casualties of the evening before finally honing in on me.

I lay down the guitar and make my way toward the entrance. Everette's still filming until I'm right up on him. He jerks the camera down to waist level and points it at me like it's an Uzi.

"What are you up to, Everette?" I say.

He grins at me, though it's one of those grins that is one part malice and one part nervous, like a politician being asked to explain a hundred thousand dollars in small bills he recently deposited in the bank.

"We're just getting some additional evidence as to your parental fitness."

"I don't see no we," I say. "Just one old meddling fool who, if he still had one, should have his ass kicked."

"Don't you be threatening me, Devon," Everette says. "I might just start this camcorder up again and get some more incriminating evidence."

"And I just might take that camcorder and perform a colonoscopy on you with it. Your daughter doesn't seem to have a problem spending the money I make here."

"What's the problem, Devon?" Hubert says, walking over from the bar.

"This man's working for *National Geographic*," I tell Hubert. "They're doing a show on primitive societies, claiming people like us are the missing link between apes and humans."

"That's a lie," Everette says, his eyes on Hubert's ball bat.

"And that's only *part* of what this footage is for," I say. "This asshole's selling what the *Geographic* doesn't want to the Moral Majority. They'll shut this place down like it's a toxic waste site."

"We don't allow no filming in here," Hubert says, taking the camcorder from Everette's hands.

Hubert jerks out the tape and douses it with the half-drunk Terminator he's been sipping. Hubert strikes a match and drops the tape on the floor. In five seconds the tape looks like black Jell-O.

Everette starts backing out the door.

"You ain't heard the last of this, Devon," he vows.

Rodney lifts a bullhorn from under the bar and announces it's one forty-five and anybody who wants a last drink had better get it now. There are few takers, most customers now lacking money or consciousness. I'm thinking to finish up with Steve Earle's "Graveyard Shift" and Dwight Yoakam's "A Thousand Miles from Nowhere," but the drunk who's been using a pool of vomit for a pillow the last hour lifts his head. He fumbles a lighter out of his pocket and flicks it on.

"Free Bird," he grunts, and lays his head back in the vomit.

And I'm thinking, why not. Ronnie Van Zant didn't have the talent of Gary Stewart or Steve Earle or Dwight Yoakam, but he did what he could with what he had. Skynyrd never pruned their Southern musical roots to give them "national appeal," and that gave their music, whatever else its failings, an honesty and an edge.

So I take out the slide from my jean pocket and start that long wailing solo for probably the millionth time in my life. I'm on automatic pilot, letting my fingers take care of business while my mind roams elsewhere.

Heads rise from tables and stare my way. Conversations stop. Couples arguing or groping each other pause as well. And this is the way it always is, as though Van Zant somehow found a conduit into the collective unconscious of his race. Whatever it is, they become serious and reflective. Maybe it's just the music's slow surging build. Or maybe something more—a yearning for the kind of freedom Van Zant's lyrics deal with, a recognition of the human need to lay their burdens down. And maybe, for a few moments, being connected to the music and lyrics enough to actually feel unshackled, free and in flight.

As I finish "Free Bird" Rodney cuts on every light in the building, including some high-beam John Deere tractor lights he's rigged on the ceiling. It's like the last scene in a vampire movie. People start wailing and whimpering. They cover their eyes, crawl under tables, and ultimately—and this is the goal—scurry toward the door and out into the dark, dragging the passed-out and knocked-out with them.

I'm off the clock now, but I don't take off my guitar and unplug the amp. Instead, I play the opening chords to Elvis Costello's "Waiting for the End of the World." Costello has tried to be the second coming of Perry Como of late, but his first two albums were pure rage and heartbreak. Those first nights after my wife and child left, I listened to Costello and it helped. Not much, but at least a little.

Hal is draped over his drum set, passed out, and Bobo is headed out the door with the big woman in the purple jumpsuit. Sammy's still on the floor so I'm flying solo.

I can't remember all the lyrics, so except for the refrain it's like I'm speaking in tongues, but it's two A.M. in western Carolina, and not much of anything makes sense. All you can do is pick up your guitar and play.

Which is what I'm doing. I'm laying down some mean guitar licks, and though I'm not much of a singer I'm giving all I got, and although The Last Chance is almost completely empty now that's okay as well because I'm merging the primal and existential and I've cranked up the volume so loud empty beer bottles are vibrating off tables and the tractor beams are pulsing like strobe lights and whatever rough beast is asleep out there in the dark is getting its wake-up call and I'm ready and waiting for whatever it's got.

LINCOLNITES

ily sat on the porch, the day's plowing done and her year-old child asleep in his crib. In her hands, the long steel needles clicked together and spread apart in a rhythmic sparring as yarn slowly unspooled from the deep pocket of her gingham dress, became part of the coverlet draped over her knees. Except for the occasional glance down the valley, Lily kept her eyes closed. She inhaled the aroma of fresh-turned earth and dogwood blossoms. She listened to the bees humming around their box. Like the fluttering she'd begun to feel in her stomach, all bespoke the return of life after a hard winter. Lily thought again of the Washington newspaper Ethan had brought with him when he'd come back from Tennessee on his Christmas furlough, how it said the war would be over by summer. Ethan had thought even sooner, claiming soon as the roads were passable Grant would take Richmond and it would be done. Good as over now, he'd told her, but Ethan had still slept in the root cellar every night of the furlough and stayed inside during the day, his haversack and rifle by the back door, because Confederates came up the valley from Boone looking for Lincolnites like Ethan.

She felt the afternoon light on her face, soothing as the hum of the bees. It was good to finally be sitting, only her hands working, the child she'd set in the shade as she'd plowed now nursed and asleep. After a few more minutes, Lily allowed her hands to rest as well, laying the foot-long needles lengthways on her lap. Reason enough to be tired, she figured, a day breaking ground with a bull-tongue plow and draft horse. Soon enough the young one would wake and she'd have to suckle him again, then fix herself something to eat as well. After that she'd need to feed the chickens and hide the horse in the woods above the spring. Lily felt the flutter again deep in her belly and knew it was another reason for her tiredness. She laid a hand on her stomach and felt the slight curve. She counted the months since Ethan's furlough and figured she'd be rounding the homespun of her dress in another month.

Lily looked down the valley to where the old Boone toll road followed Middlefork Creek. Her eyes closed once more as she mulled over names for the coming child, thinking about how her own birthday was also in September and that by then Ethan would be home for good and they'd be a family again, the both of them young enough not to be broken by the hardships of the last two years. Lily made a picture in her mind of her and Ethan and the young ones all together, the crops she'd planted ripe and proud in the field, the apple tree's branches sagging with fruit.

When she opened her eyes, the Confederate was in the yard. He must have figured she'd be watching the road because he'd come down Goshen Mountain instead, emerging from a thick stand of birch trees he'd followed down the creek. It was too late to hide the horse and gather the chickens into the root cellar, too late to go get the butcher knife and conceal it in her dress pocket, so Lily just watched him approach, a musket in his right hand and a tote sack in the left. He wore a threadbare butternut jacket and a cap. A strip of cowhide held up a pair of ragged wool trousers. Only the boots looked new. Lily knew the man those boots had belonged to, and she knew the hickory tree where they'd left the rest of him dangling, not only a rope around his neck but also a cedar shingle with the word *Lincolnite* burned into the wood.

The Confederate grinned as he stepped into the yard. He raised a finger and thumb to the cap, but his eyes were on the chickens scratching for worms behind the barn, the draft horse in the pasture. He looked to be about forty, though in these times people often looked older than they were, even children. The Confederate wore his cap brim tilted high, his face tanned to the hue of cured tobacco. Not the way a farmer would wear a hat or cap. The gaunt face and loose-fitting trousers made clear what the tote sack was for. Lily hoped a couple of chickens were enough for him, but the boots did not reassure her of that.

"Afternoon," he said, letting his gaze settle on Lily briefly before looking westward toward Grandfather Mountain. "Looks to be some rain coming, maybe by full dark."

"Take what chickens you want," Lily said. "I'll help you catch them."

"I plan on that," he said.

The man raised his left forearm and wiped sweat off his brow, the tote sack briefly covering his face. As he lowered his arm, his grin had been replaced with a seeming sobriety.

"But it's also my sworn duty to requisition that draft horse for the cause."

"For the cause," Lily said, meeting his eyes, "like them boots you're wearing."

The Confederate set a boot onto the porch step as though to better examine it.

"These boots wasn't requisitioned. Traded my best piece of rope for them, but I'm of a mind you already know that." He raised his eyes and looked at Lily. "That neighbor of yours wasn't as careful on his furlough as your husband."

Lily studied the man's face, a familiarity behind the scraggly beard and the hard unflinching gaze. She thought back to the time a man or woman from up here could go into Boone. A time when disagreement over what politicians did down in Raleigh would be settled in this county with, at worst, clenched fists.

"You used to work at Old Man Mast's store, didn't you?" Lily said.

"I did," the Confederate said.

"My daddy used to trade with you. One time when I was with him you give me and my sister a peppermint."

The man's eyes didn't soften, but something in his face seemed to let go a little, just for a moment.

"Old Mast didn't like me doing that, but it was a small enough thing to do for the chaps."

For a few moments he didn't say anything else, maybe thinking back to that time, maybe not.

"Your name was Mr. Vaughn," Lily said. "I remember that now."

The Confederate nodded.

"It still is," he said, "my name being Vaughn, I mean."
He paused. "But that don't change nothing in the here
and now, though, does it?"

"No," Lily replied. "I guess it don't."

"So I'll be taking the horse," Vaughn said, "lest you
got something to barter for it, maybe some of that Yankee money they pay your man with over in Tennessee?
We might could make us a trade for some of that."

"There ain't no money here," Lily said, telling the
truth because what money they had she'd sewn in
Ethan's coat lining. Safer there than anywhere on the
farm, she'd told Ethan before he left, but he'd agreed
only after she'd also sewn his name and where to send
his body on the coat's side pocket. Ethan's older brother
had done the same, the two of them vowing to get the
other's coat home if not the body.

"I guess I better get to it then," Vaughn said, "try to
beat this rain back to Boone."

He turned from her, whistling "Dixie" as he walked
toward the pasture, almost to the split-rail fence when
Lily told him she had something to trade for the horse.

"What would that be?" Vaughn asked.

Lily lifted the ball of thread off her lap and placed it
on the porch's puncheon floor, then set the half-finished
coverlet on the floor as well. As she got up from the
chair, her hands smoothed the gingham around her

hips. Lily stepped to the porch edge and freed the braid so her blonde hair fell loose on her neck and shoulders.

"You know my meaning," she said.

Vaughn stepped onto the porch, not speaking as he did so. To look her over, Lily knew. She sucked in her stomach slightly to conceal her condition, though his knowing she was with child might make it better for him. A man could think that way in these times, she thought. Lily watched as Vaughn silently mulled over his choices, including the choice he'd surely come to by now that he could just as easily have her and the horse both.

"How old are you?" he asked.

"Nineteen."

"Nineteen," Vaughn said, though whether this was or wasn't in her favor she did not know. He looked west again toward Grandfather Mountain and studied the sky before glancing down the valley at the toll road.

Okay," he finally said, and nodded toward the front door. "Let's you and me go inside."

"Not in the cabin," Lily answered. "My young one's in there."

For a moment she thought Vaughn would insist, but he didn't.

"Where then?"

"The root cellar. It's got a pallet we can lay on."

Vaughn's chin lifted, his eyes seeming to focus on something behind Lily and the chair.

"I reckon we'll know where to look for your man next time, won't we?" When Lily didn't respond, Vaughn offered a smile that looked almost friendly. "Lead on," he said.

Vaughn followed her around the cabin, past the bee box and chopping block and the old root cellar, the one they'd used before the war. They followed the faintest path through a thicket of rhododendron until it ended abruptly on a hillside. Lily cleared away the green-leaved rhododendron branches she replaced each week and unlatched a square wooden door. The hinges creaked as the entrance yawned open, the root cellar's damp earthy odor mingling with the smell of the dogwood blossoms. The afternoon sun revealed an earthen floor lined with jars of vegetables and honey, at the center a pallet and quilt. There were no steps, just a three-foot drop.

"And you think me stupid enough to go in there first?" Vaughn said.

"I'll go in first," Lily answered, and sat down in the entrance, dangling one foot until it touched the packed earth. She held to the door frame and eased herself inside, crouching low, trying not to think how she might be stepping into her own grave. The corn shucks rasped beneath her as she settled on the pallet.

"We could do it as easy up here," Vaughn said, peering at her from the entrance. "It's good as some old spider hole."

"I ain't going to dirty myself rooting around on the ground," Lily said.

She thought he'd leave the musket outside, but instead Vaughn buckled his knees and leaned, set his left hand on a beam. As he shifted his body to enter, Lily took the metal needles from her dress pocket and laid them behind her.

Vaughn set his rifle against the earthen wall and hunched to take off his coat and unknot the strip of cowhide around his pants. The sunlight made his face appear dark and featureless as if in silhouette. As he moved closer, Lily shifted to the left side of the mattress to make room for him. Lily smelled tobacco on his breath as he pulled his shirt up to his chest and lay down on his back, fingers already fumbling to free his trouser buttons. His sunken belly was so white compared to his face and drab clothing it seemed to glow in the strained light. Lily took one of the needles into her hand. She thought of the hog she'd slaughtered last January, remembering how the liver wrapped itself around the stomach, like a saddle. Not so much difference in a hog's guts and a man's, she'd heard one time.

"Shuck off that dress or raise it," Vaughn said, his fingers on the last button. "I ain't got time to dawdle."

"All right," Lily said, hiking up her hem before kneeling beside him.

She reached behind and grasped the needle. When

Vaughn placed his thumbs between cloth and hips to pull down his trousers, Lily raised her right arm and fell forward, her left palm set against the needle's rounded stem so the steel wouldn't slip through her fingers. She plunged the steel as deep as she could. When the needle stalled a moment on the backbone, Lily pushed harder and the needle point scraped past bone and went the rest of the way through. She felt the smooth skin of Vaughn's belly and flattened both palms over the needle's stem. Pin him to the floor if you can, she told herself, pushing out the air in Vaughn's stomach as the needle point pierced the root cellar's packed dirt.

Vaughn's hands stayed on his trousers a moment longer, as though not yet registering what had happened. Lily scrambled to the entrance while Vaughn shifted his forearms and slowly raised his head. He stared at the needle's rounded stem that pressed into his flesh like a misplaced button. His legs pulled inward toward his hips, but he seemed unable to move his midsection, as if the needle had indeed pinned him to the floor. Lily took the rifle and set it outside, then pulled herself out of the hole as Vaughn loosed a long lowing moan.

She watched from above, waiting to see if she'd need to figure out how to use the musket. After almost a minute, Vaughn's mouth grimaced, the teeth locking together like a dog tearing meat. He pushed himself backward with his forearms until he was able to slump his head and shoulders against the dirt wall. Lily could hear his breaths and see the rise of his chest. His eyes moved, looking her way now. Lily did not know if Vaughn could actually see her. He raised his right hand a few inches off the root cellar's floor, palm upward as he stretched his arm toward the entrance, as if to catch what light leaked in from the world. Lily closed and latched the cellar door, covered the entrance with the rhododendron branches before walking back to the cabin.

The child was awake and fretting. Lily went to the crib but before taking up the boy she pulled back the bedding and removed the butcher knife, placed it in her dress pocket. She nursed the child and then fixed herself a supper of cornbread and beans. As Lily ate, she wondered if the Confederate had told anyone in Boone where he was headed. Maybe, but probably he wouldn't have said which particular farm, wouldn't have known himself which one until he found something to take. Ponder something else, she told herself, and thought again of names for the coming child. Girl names, because Granny Triplett had already rubbed Lily's belly and told her this one would be a girl. Lily said those she'd considered out loud and again settled on Mary, because it would be the one to match her boy's name.

After she'd cleared the table and changed the child's swaddlings, Lily set him in the crib and went outside,

scattering shell corn for the chickens before walking back through the rhododendron to the root cellar.
There was less light now, and when she peered though
the slats in the wood door she could see just enough to
make out Vaughn's body slumped against the earthen
wall. Lily watched several minutes for any sign of
movement, listened for a moan, a sigh, the exhalation
of a breath. Only then did she slowly unlatch the door.
Lily opened it a few inches at a time until she could
see clearly. Vaughn's chin rested on his chest, his legs
splayed out before him. The needle was still in his stomach, every bit as deep as before. His face was white as his
belly now, bleached looking. She quietly closed the door
and latched it softly, as if a noise might startle Vaughn
back to life. Lily gathered the rhododendron branches
and concealed the entrance.

She sat on the porch with the child and watched the
dark settle in the valley. A last barn swallow swept low
across the pasture and into the barn as the first drops of
rain began to fall, soft and hesitant at first, then less so.
Lily went inside, taking the coverlet and yarn with her.
She lit the lamp and nursed the child a last time and put
him back in the crib. The supper fire still smoldered in
the hearth, giving some warmth against the evening's
chill. It was the time of evening when she'd usually knit
some more, but since she couldn't do that tonight Lily
took the newspaper from under the mattress and sat

down at the table. She read the article again about the war being over by summer, stumbling over a few words that she didn't know. When she came to the word *Abraham*, she glanced over at the crib. Not too long before I can call him by his name to anyone, Lily told herself.

After a while longer, she hid the newspaper again and lay down in the bed. The rain was steady now on the cabin's cedar shingles. The young one breathed steadily in the crib beside the bed. Rain hard, she thought, thinking of what she'd be planting first when daylight came. Bad as it was that it had happened in the first place, there'd been some luck in it too. At least it wasn't winter when the ground was hard as granite. She could get it done by noon, especially after a soaking rain, then rest a while before doing her inside chores, maybe even have time to plant some tomato and squash before supper.

ACKNOWLEDGMENTS

Thanks to my editor, Lee Boudreaux, and my agent, Marly Rusoff. Thanks also to Abigail Holstein, Mihai Rădulescu, Western Carolina University, and my family.